A NOVEL OF LOVE AND INTRIGUE

# *Passage to Peru*

A NOVEL OF LOVE AND INTRIGUE

# Passage to Peru

## MARIE AVANT

**WinePress Publishing**
**MUKILTEO, WA 98275**

# DEDICATION

To my husband Marshall whose love, encouragement and support, along with the knowledge he shared, enabled me to write this inspirational novel.

To Sallie E. Stuart for her helpful critiques.

To Gayle Roper for her suggestions to enhance the novel.

To Nola Love for her faith in my ability to complete the work.

To all those friends who urged me to get written.

# CONTENTS

# PROLOGUE

What happens when an impulsive, determined young civil engineer, who feels he is invulnerable and starts after what he wants, then fails to reach his goal because life tosses in a few challenges such as when his plane is shot down the third time in the South Pacific and he is hospitalized several months for recovery and therapy. Later returns to South America, becomes successful enough to own a construction company and acquire jungle land, when a new government comes into power, takes over and nationalizes foreign businesses and he loses everything?

He returns to the United States, the land of his birth, broke. Despite his losses, he has a strong desire to someday go back to work in those beautiful countries; hire workers from the poorer class who want to help themselves rise above their poverty.

Perhaps it is the crisis of losing everything overnight that causes him to realize he must be willing to change if he is to reach his goal of returning to South America the second time to work and help the lower class to help themselves. He must trust God's timing and guidance for his life.

How he feels about his losses:  a country, people, the woman he planned to marry, begins this novel of love and intrigue.

# CHAPTER ONE

Jay Ryan stomped into the international airport of Lima, Peru with a pained expression on his face and eyes that betrayed the anger and hurt he felt. Pushing past a noisy group by the door, he made his way to the ticket counter. Bracing his short, muscular body against it, he let his luggage drop to the floor and stared unseeing into the distance. It was seven A.M., another hour until his departure.

He scanned the crowd that was milling around while they, too, waited to leave. They were professionals like him. People who had spent years in the country and spoke fluent Spanish. As he studied their faces, he thought they looked as if they had lost loved ones. He could relate to them. Not only had he lost a country he loved and a people he cared for, but also the woman he loved and planned to marry.

It was strange how circumstances had made such a drastic change in his life. Losing his possessions and land was one thing, but deciding not to marry Antonita troubled him and disturbed his sleep.

How kind Enrique had been to take him to the home of Antonita and her parents the night before. He was glad he got to spend a few moments with her and tell her good-by.

Her arms had closed tightly around him as she cried, "I can't let you go. You're my life!"

"Antonita, you don't understand. I've lost everything, I'm broke!"

"No problem," said Antonita, shrugging her shoulders. "After my parents give us a lovely wedding, we'll live with them until you find a job."

"Antonita, I wouldn't be happy letting your parents support us."

"Why not? They already love you and treat you like a son."

"Perhaps so, but how long would they be pleased with the situation if I couldn't get a job here?"

Jay remembered looking into her dark eyes that implored him to stay and hearing her whisper "I love you." He now struggled with his thoughts. Would he later regret his decision to return to the United States?

Antonita's sobbing touched his heart. Holding her in the circle of his arms, he said, "I *must* go. If God wills, I'll return to South America." His eyes misty, he kissed her and walked out.

En route to Jay's hotel, Enrique remarked, "Until you find the right one, there's no way of knowing how many women you will almost marry. If you weren't leaving the country, I think you'd marry Antonita."

"True. I cared for her, but I had nothing to offer after I lost everything. Even though she suggested it, I couldn't let her parents support us. She is accustomed to living in a modern city with conveniences. Once she roughed it with me in more primitive areas, she would've become discouraged and returned to her parents, leaving me a lonely, heartbroken man."

"You're right, she's used to the best of everything. Perhaps it was not meant for you to marry her," said Enrique. "By the way, whatever happened to the attractive English nurse you planned to marry?"

"I don't know. After a brief visit with her parents in Peru, she left to work in a London hospital. I looked for her when I was stationed in England, but I never found her."

"Been a long while, hasn't it?" asked Enrique.

"I last saw her in 1943 when I came up from Chile. She said she wasn't free to marry because of an obligation to her country. So after I returned to Santiago, I went to the American Embassy and volunteered for the American Air Force."

The two friends left off talking until Enrique broke the silence.

"I hate to see you troubled, Jay. Wish I could help you."

"You already have, more than you know. I guess I'm hurt and disappointed by how things turned out and what's happened to me as a result. As if it wasn't enough for the new government to nationalize foreign businesses and take over my company, they also insisted I finish paving the city's new subdivision before I leave."

"Did they pay you?" Enrique asked.

"Not unless you consider payment to be my plane ticket and the one piece of luggage I'm allowed to take," said Jay.

"I'm sorry for your misfortune, but thanks to God you're alive. With your skills and experience, you'll make out, Jay."

"Yeah, you're right. I shouldn't complain," said Jay, sighing.

Later at the hotel, Enrique said, "I'll take you to the airport in the morning."

"Thanks, I'd appreciate it." Jay hopped out and waved to him before going inside.

As he crawled into bed, he wrestled with his thoughts. Had he made the right decision regarding Antonita? If he had stayed, he might have found an engineering job in a neighboring country, but would she have been content living in the remote places where he worked? He also recalled her father telling him, "If you marry our daughter, her mother and I hope you'll stay closeby so we can see her often."

Though it hurt to walk away from Antonita, he believed it was better for them both. She had a dynamic personality and was the most beautiful woman he had ever met. It would not be easy to forget her.

When Enrique came for him the next morning, Jay said, "You're like a brother to me."

"I know," said Enrique, "you're the same for me. Do you plan to return someday?"

"Yes, I do. I hope to get a good engineering job in the States, save my money, and come back to work in one of these beautiful countries. I'll start my own company and hire poor people who are eager to work to improve their quality of life."

"May I live to see that day," said Enrique, smiling.

As Enrique left him at the airport and drove away, Jay realized how much he was going to miss his friend. Lost in thought and reliving precious moments, he jumped when the ticket agent called, "Señor! Your ticket."

"Thanks," Jay mumbled and went to sit down.

"See you survived," an American businessman said as he moved over to make room for Jay.

"Yeah. Tough situation. As a result of the nationalization and take over, I lost more than two million dollars."

"Wow! How'd you lose so much?"

"My construction company and equipment, along with the jungle land I was developing into a coffee plantation. After I built houses for the poor families I'd hired, a subversive group from another area came while I was away and killed them all, destroyed their homes, then dynamited the runway I used to bring in supplies."

"Good thing you were gone."

"Yes, had I been there they'd have killed me too," Jay said. "Who would have thought it possible? It was a real shocker to fly over the site afterward and see the destruction."

"Yeah, terrible for innocent people to lose their lives when you were trying to help them. I sort of expected a change in the government, so a while ago I began sending money to a bank in my hometown. Once I reach the States, I'm going into the landscaping business."

"I'd sure be in better shape financially if I'd followed your plan. Thanks to a friend's advice, I sent a few thousand dollars to a bank in Los Angeles, but it won't last long. What I'm having a hard time accepting is how fast my social status has changed."

"Yeah, being financially independent, then losing everything and your means to earn a living is enough to send anybody into shock," the man agreed.

While they were busy talking, they failed to hear the bilingual announcement, "Plane bound for the United Sates is ready for boarding. Last call for boarding the plane to the United States!"

The two jumped up, raced across the terminal, and rushed out the door to get on the plane.

Jay got his seat belt fastened as the captain began revving the DC6's motors in readiness for take off. When they became airborne, he looked out at the city. His eyes brimmed with tears at the possibility of never seeing it or Antonita again. What would his life have been like had he married her? They had very little in common. She was a lovely, educated young woman from a prominent family and social class. He had grown up in a primitive section of Peru and had learned to relate to people without giving a second thought to their socioeconomic class or color.

Glancing at the Andes Mountains, he recalled the morning he had ridden Cayuse, his pony, along a trail between the canyon walls. Watching condors in their nests up on high ledges, he forgot danger until the pony trembled and backed up onto a narrow trail. One misstep would have resulted in the two of them falling to their deaths on the canyon floor below. Then the cougar vanished and reappeared on the opposite side of the canyon.

It was strange how childhood memories, incidents he had long since forgotten, flashed across his mind now. Daring and curious to know the world around him, he had always welcomed high adventure without regard for its consequences or danger.

Amid the hushed voices on the plane, he realized his tense body felt like a frayed rubber band ready to break. Too weary to keep his eyes open, he fell asleep.

He had not been sleeping long when the stewardess asked, "Breakfast, Sir?"

"Yes, please," he mumbled, struggling to wake up.

Turning to the well-dressed gentleman sitting next to him, he said, "Let's introduce ourselves before we eat. My name is Jay Ryan."

"I'm Ramiro Cortez. Call me Ramiro."

"Pleased to meet you, Ramiro. Now that we've met we can enjoy our breakfast. Smelling those scrambled eggs and sausages has made me hungry."

For the next hour they concentrated on their food and made occasional small talk until the stewardess came for their trays.

Jay said, "I grew up in South America."

"Interesting. Were your parents missionaries?"

"No, my father was a civil engineer and he accepted a job with an American company in Bolivia. I'm also a civil engineer. I graduated from the National University School of Engineering in Santiago, Chile."

"I earned my degree from the same university," said Ramiro.

"You're kidding," said Jay.

"True. My father's cousin was a professor at the university and he advised my parents to send me there when I was ready for college. I liked the area and have continued to live near the city since I graduated. But enough about me. Where did you grow up?"

"In Peru."

"Then what caused you to choose Chile for your engineering training?"

"I had finished my second year at the University of Texas, when I received notice of a test being given. The top ten applicants who came to Santiago to take the test would get an all-expenses-paid, five-year scholarship. At the time, I was in Peru staying at my parents' home in Cuzco. It sounded good, so I took the three-day train trip down to Santiago."

"And you passed?" asked Ramiro.

"Yes, and I also settled the problem of which university I'd attend. It would have been an excellent choice, even if I hadn't won the scholarship. The on-the-job training I got while working two summer vacations with a Chilean construction company was an added benefit. This led to a job with a Peruvian construction company with several contracts in the Andes Mountains to build roads and irrigation channels. After graduation, I formed my own company. I did well and bought some jungle land, which I recently lost, along with my construction company."

"You're not married, are you, Jay?"

"No. I've been a wanderer working in different countries. Whenever I got interested in settling down in one place, something always changed my plans. If I hadn't lost everything in the recent takeover, I'd be getting ready to marry a Peruvian woman."

"Don't you believe she'd have been happy marrying you even if you were broke?"

"Perhaps so, if I'd agreed to stay in Peru and let her parents support us until I got a job. After struggling for a week to find the answer and seeing my future as being rather dismal, I decided to return to the States and leave the field to her other suitors. Before that I was engaged to an English nurse I'd known for years. During the war, she felt she had a commitment to help England and didn't feel free to marry me. So, I volunteered for the American Air Force at the American Embassy in Santiago."

"Why did you choose the air force?"

"I soloed at sixteen and liked flying"

"Guess you saw plenty of action," said Ramiro.

"As a fighter pilot serving in Europe, my job was to protect our big bombers. My plane got hit several times, but I always got back to base. When things slowed down on the European front, I was sent home for a week's leave before being shipped out to the South Pacific."

"Did you contact the young nurse while you were in England?"

"No luck. Whenever I got a three-day pass, I spent my time going from one boardinghouse to the next, but I always got the same answer. They said she had moved and left no forwarding address. However, honoring my commitment to try to find her probably saved my life."

"How was that?"

"An elderly lady at a boardinghouse where she first stayed told me to check back with her later. I thought she might have some information to help me locate her. On my last afternoon in London, I went back and found she wasn't home. I returned to the hotel where I was supposed to wait for my ride to the base, when an air raid sounded. I ran to the nearest shelter. After the attack and the all-clear, I rushed back to the hotel and found it blown to pieces, nothing but a smoldering crater."

"You're lucky to be alive. Did the driver get through to you, Jay?"

"Not at that moment. He was nowhere near the hotel. I waited three hours hoping he might make it. When he failed to show, I knew it was up to me to get out of London and return to base. I headed toward the city's outskirts.

"You'd never believe the trouble I ran into that night with the blackout, streets torn up, and chuck holes of varying sizes and depths left from earlier bombing raids. I fell into more than my quota, before I learned to proceed slowly and feel my way. Worst of all was the cold, thick fog that crept in and hovered over me like a burial shroud. After walking for hours and ending up back where I started, I realized I had circled around.

"There was nothing else to do but keep going. I plodded along through the night. Numbed by the cold, my legs felt like they were covered with layers of ice. I kept going until out of the night a truck slowed and someone shouted, 'Need a ride?' I gratefully accepted the offer, then struggled to lift my feet high enough to climb inside. Only then did I recognize the driver who was supposed to pick me up at the hotel."

"Marvelous! How did he know he'd find you walking along the street?"

"He believed I had been killed in the blast while waiting for him at the hotel. He did not expect to find me. Actually, after all my wandering I was still near the hotel site when he stopped to give me a ride. Since I had made such little progress, he joked and said, 'At the rate you were traveling, the war could end while you're getting out of London.' Some call it luck that my life was spared. I call it God's protection."

"What about your commander? Was he surprised to see you?"

"He said, 'Captain, I'm glad to see you back and walking in one piece.'"

"Such a miserable night. I'll bet you were ready to sleep," said Ramiro.

"Are you serious? I hardly finished my report when the alert sounded over the intercom, 'All available pilots report to the briefing room.' After receiving our instructions, we jumped onto the personnel carrier to ride out to our planes and off we went to fight again."

"From what I've read, I imagine fighting in the South Pacific was quite different."

"Yes. Sometimes I flew hundreds of miles to a U.S. Carrier in order to resupply gasoline, oil, and ammunition. It was during this period that a meal might be a hamburger eaten on the run with no time for a shower. Various islands were won and lost during fierce aerial battles. My plane, a P48, was shot down twice during two of them. I managed to have it repaired and get into battle again."

"It's amazing you survived being shot down twice," said Ramiro.

"Yes, but I was less fortunate a few days later when my plane was shot down for the third time. Unable to continue fighting, I radioed the commander, 'I've been hit. I'm badly wounded and leaving the battle for base.' 'Good luck!' radioed the commander."

"And you crashed?"

"No. I'd been shot in the lungs and stomach and was bleeding profusely, but I kept flying until I reached a small airstrip with a dirt runway. I made a rough landing, and managed to switch off the plane's motors to prevent it catching fire before I blacked out. It was the following day when I came to and saw a doctor standing by my cot. He said, 'You must be made of steel to survive what you've been through. We're readying you for flight to a hospital ship and then on to a hospital in the United States.'"

"Jay, it must have taken months to recover."

"It did. The war ended while I was still a patient. Then there were several months of therapy at another place."

"How depressing for you."

"It was at first. Then as time passed and I began to regain my strength, I dreamed of returning to work on a challenging engineering job in the Andes Mountains of South America." Jay stifled a yawn. "Ramiro, I can't stay awake. I need a nap."

"Go ahead," said Ramiro. "I'll review my seminar presentation for El Paso."

It seemed to Jay he had hardly closed his eyes when Ramiro called his name.

"Here's lunch. It looks good."

"I'm awake," Jay said, rubbing his eyes and yawning.

They didn't talk while they ate. The minute they finished and put their trays aside, Ramiro asked, "Was all your schooling in Chile?"

"No. I attended a mission school in Peru until I was ready for high school. It was two days on horseback from our ranch to the nearest town and to the school I attended. My parents enrolled me when I was six years old. The first year I was there they came once a month to see me. I loved my parents and missed them terribly. Being separated from them for weeks at a time was hard for me to accept."

"Tell me, what was the closest town to your mission school, Jay?"

"Urco. A Quechua word."

Smiling, Ramiro said, "It's possible we may have attended the same school in Peru. My father was killed in a car accident when I was five. My mother and I went to live with my maternal grandparents on their ranch a few miles from the mission. When I was six, my mother and my grandparents took me there and I began learning to speak English. Grandfather had Manuel, a ranch worker, take me by horseback to classes. After one year, my grandparents bought a townhouse in the city and we moved there."

"Some of my happiest memories are those of the mission school, living on our ranch, and learning Quechua from friends who were descendants of the Inca. I spent days and sometimes nights in their village, and they took turns staying in my home."

"Jay, I know you've lived an exciting life in those primitive areas on your father's ranch. Would you share something from your childhood?"

"Sure. One I'll always remember is the dark night I traveled over the 1,600-feet-high pass between our ranch and a small town. Dad got sick and needed medicine we could only get at a small pharmacy there. I told the cook where I was going, but asked her not to tell Dad I had gone. I saddled our strongest riding horse and left. I relaxed and let the horse find his way along the trail until I heard men's voices. I had come upon a band of cattle rustlers gathered around a small campfire. They pointed their guns my way and planned to shoot me as I came closer. Then their leader shouted, 'He's a kid! Let him go!'"

"Think you'll return to South America in the future?"

"I hope the day will come. I've grown up, lived, and worked in all those beautiful countries. I'd like to help poor people the way I did before. Do you know I hired as many as four hundred men on a job? Since we were working in areas where game was plentiful, I provided them with meat every day. When I worked near a village, I made roads from their village to the main road and it did not cost them anything. This made it easier for them to travel and take their wares to market in the city."

The stewardess arrived with refreshments. As he sipped his tomato juice, he asked, "How much flight time do we have left?"

"We've been in the air six hours. It's at least another hour or more," she replied.

As she walked away, Ramiro said, "Jay, I want to thank you for helping to make this flight such a pleasant one for me. It's been great talking with you and exchanging our experiences. If you get back to Santiago, call me. I'd like you to meet my family."

"Thanks, I will. I feel better now than when I boarded the plane. This morning my future looked bleak because I was dwelling on what I'd lost, rather than on what I have: my health and experience in the engineering field. You've been a terrific listener. Talking with you has helped me more than you know."

"It was good for both of us, Jay. I'm glad you introduced yourself."

"Will you be catching your flight to El Paso as soon as we land?"

"No," said Ramiro. "I'm spending a couple of days with my cousin and his family."

"I wish you a pleasant visit, a successful business trip, and safe return home."

As soon as they stopped talking, they heard the captain's voice over the intercom, "Attention all passengers: We'll be landing at the International Airport in Los Angeles in approximately thirty minutes. Secure your seat belts and please observe the nonsmoking signs."

The DC6 made a smooth landing and taxied down the runway to the terminal. Jay joined the other passengers hurrying toward the baggage claim. He paused a moment to reflect on the differences between this country and the one he had left: the priceless freedoms that he and other United States citizens accepted and took for granted.

At five P.M. he picked up his luggage and asked a cab driver to take him to a cheap motel.

After driving through what looked to be the worst part of town, the driver turned down a narrow alley and stopped in front of the crummiest looking motel Jay had seen in any country. Cardboard replaced broken glass in the front windows, making the building look as if it would welcome an earthquake to put it to rest.

"Here you are," said the driver.

"Wait a minute. When I said 'cheap,' I didn't mean something like this."

"Okay, I gotcha. We're looking for reasonable—not cheap. I know just the place."

"Thanks," Jay said with a sigh, as he began to calm down.

"You new in Los Angeles?" the driver asked.

"Yes."

"If you want, I can point out the sights."

"I'd appreciate it," said Jay.

True to his word, the driver spouted an endless travelogue as they worked their way through rush-hour traffic.

"Did you grow up in Los Angeles?" Jay asked.

"No, I'm a Nebraska farm boy. I decided to move to California when I graduated from high school. My folks didn't have much money, so I walked and hitched rides to get here. I showed up with little more than a dream and a lot of faith in God."

"As far as I'm concerned, that's all you need," Jay said with a smile.

"I found work I could do and I've never been without a paying job. I own my cab and it's paid for. Wife and I own our home, too."

Enjoying the tour, Jay had not realized that an hour had passed until he glanced at his watch. The driver turned down a tree-lined street leading to a motel. When he parked in front of the office entrance, Jay asked, "Reasonable, not cheap?"

"Yeah, Sipes Motel. Come meet the owners, Ned and Grace Sipes. Good people."

Jay followed him into the tidy lobby where an older man greeted them. After making some introductions, he asked,"What can we do for you?"

"I'd like a room," Jay told him.

"Will you be staying more than one night?"

"Yes, a week or longer."

"Fine. Let me show you what we have," he said, leading the way. Impressed with what he saw, Jay chose the one which resembled a comfortable family room. It was perfect for relaxing, forgetting past hurts and beginning again.

After he registered, the driver said, "I'm Ben Baskom. If there's more you want to see tomorrow, I'm available."

"How about stopping by at eight tomorrow morning? I need to find a place that does résumés and helps people find jobs."

"Sure. I'll be here."

Jay went to his room, stretched out on the bed and began reviewing events of the day. What began as the worst one he could recall in recent memory, had turned out a lot better. Even if his future appeared less than promising at the moment, he trusted God to lead him. Thinking pleasant thoughts, he relaxed and went to sleep.

# CHAPTER TWO

The next morning, Jay awoke at six o'clock feeling anything but rested. He had spent most of the night tossing and turning reliving his last weeks in Peru. What was there about the country and its people that gave him such a strong desire to return? Was it due to his parents' death and their burial in Peru? Could it be Antonita? Perhaps, for there were moments it took all his will power to put memory of her aside.

He struggled with the problem past midnight then prayed, "Dear God, you know my situation and everything about me. Please help me avoid living in the past and get on with my life." Only then did he relax and fall asleep.

Accustomed to rising early without an alarm clock, he marveled that he woke up at six. He yawned and glanced across the room to where his bulging suitcase rested on a bench. Since it had refused to stay closed, he had strapped his widest leather belt around its middle. He chuckled as he recalled Enrique's remarks about it, 'Worse case of indigestion I've seen in a piece of luggage, Jay. Hope it don't "burp."'

He went over and opened it. Clothes spilled out onto the floor. He crammed them back inside, then dumped the contents on the bed. There were mementos he desired to keep — things reminding him of the happy years while his parents were living. The most cherished was his Holy Bible, a gift he'd received from the mission school for verses he'd learned. When troubled, he had often found help by reading the Bible, praying, and praising God.

He regretted his inability to find friends of his family with whom he had left a small trunk containing his important personal papers. How he wished he had thought to choose a permanent address for saving such items. An adventuresome person, he was on the move from one country to the next, and his work was often in the most remote and primitive areas. He lived out of his duffel bag with his work clothes and little else. Deciding he could not retrieve his papers and might need to find how to replace them later, he dressed and went to eat.

"Good morning. Ready for breakfast?" Ned Sipes asked as Jay took a table.

"Yes. I'd like two eggs over easy, a stack of whole wheat toast, a glass of orange juice, and a cup of coffee."

"Have any trouble sleeping your first night in our motel?" Ned asked.

"No. How did you find this quiet location?" Jay asked.

"Years ago, I figured this spot would be ideal for a family-owned motel. Property wasn't as costly as it is now," Ned explained.

"Looks as if it's been a wise investment," Jay told him.

"It has been. We have people stop by to stay with us year after year."

At that moment, Mrs. Sipes brought his food and Jay left off talking. He had almost finished eating, when Ben Baskom entered.

"Hi, Ben. Come join me. Had breakfast?"

"Yes, but I'll take a cup of coffee," Ben said, smiling, then sitting down.

"I'm in a state of shock, Ben. It dawned on me last night that I'm back in my home country but I don't know a single business person who is familiar with my skills and can give me a letter of reference. Without one, my résumés will be of little value. It's ironic to think I volunteered for the American Air Force, saw combat in both Europe and the South Pacific, yet there's no U.S. company to recommend me."

"Won't they take your references from South American countries?" asked Ben.

"Don't think so. Once I'm offered a job, I'll need to work on probation. But enough singing the blues. Let's go activate my account at First National Bank."

As they rode along, Jay admired Ben's driving skills and how he maneuvered his way through busy streets.

"It's sure great to ride with a careful driver who knows the city, yet hurries to get me where I need to go."

"Thanks. We're a couple of blocks from the bank. After I let you out at the front door, I'll park across the street and wait for you."

"Shouldn't take long to get the job done," Jay said.

Seeing the long lines waiting to be served inside, Jay guessed everyone in Los Angeles must have come to the bank at this hour. He joined the nearest one and waited. The line moved slowly. He asked a man ahead of him, "Is it like this every day?"

The man looked him over, then asked, "What country you from?"

"The United States," Jay replied.

"Not been here long, have you?"

"No, arrived yesterday afternoon around five P.M."

"I thought so. You don't talk like somebody from California."

"Give me time and I might," said Jay.

Eventually, he reached the teller's window, but was told that she was not the person who could help him. He was finally shown into an office where things were promptly taken care of, once they saw his passport and he answered some questions to prove he had sent money to them from South America.

He walked out of the bank and looked around. Ben tapped the horn. Jay saw him and crossed over.

Getting inside the cab, he said, "I should go by the State Patrol Office and get a driver's manual; but first, I want to see what's available in pickups."

"Where you wanna start?" Ben asked.

"A Chevrolet place," said Jay.

On the way, they passed a large used car lot. "That looks interesting, Ben. Let's see what they have."

Two hours later, after listening to the spiel of the salesperson and trying out the available pickups, Jay concluded that none of them met his requirements. By then it was almost noon.

Ben asked, "Wanna grab a bite to eat before tackling your next project? It's early, but I wanna take you to a small place where they make the best bean soup I've tasted, other than my wife's. After we eat, we'll be in better shape to hit other used car lots or the Chevrolet place."

"Great."

They found The Eatery was packed when they entered. They had to wait a few minutes before being seated and served.

After tasting the bean soup, Jay told Ben, "It was worth waiting for."

"Glad you like it, Jay."

They spent the afternoon going from one used car lot to the next without finding anything suitable.

Jay complained, "They all look good until I try them and find they've seen their best days. I've got to have something I can depend on."

"If you're ready to leave, Jay, we'll go to the motel and try again tomorrow."

"Before we do that, would you mind driving by the State Patrol Office so I can pick up a driver's manual to study?"

"Sure," said Ben, turning down another street.

Jay got the manual, thumbed through it, and said, "This will help me prepare for the test. Then, maybe I'll be lucky enough to find a good, used pickup. I'd also like to buy a strong tool chest I can lock and bolt to the back."

"Don't think it'll be a problem to find what you want, Jay. There are plenty of places to visit. I'll come by at the same time tomorrow and we'll see how things work out."

"Good. I'm tired enough to sleep standing up."

Ben laughed. "Better not try it," he advised.

In his room, Jay slipped off his shoes and leaned back in his comfortable chair. With his eyes closed, he wondered if he would ever get over the tiredness? What caused the occasional sharp twinges of pain along his side? Did it result from the stress of deciding if he should marry Antonita, even if there was no job in sight? He cared for her more than he realized. Had he not been such a proud, macho man, he would have had no problem moving in with her parents once they were married. He wasn't solving anything and it was only making it harder for him to forget her. He sighed and went downstairs to eat.

Soon after he ate, he returned to his room and got ready for bed. As he closed his evening prayer, he asked God to protect and guide Antonita. He fell asleep and slept until seven o'clock the next morning.

"Wow, eleven hours of rest!" he exclaimed.

He set a speed record hurrying to breakfast. He had just finished as Ben entered the dining area. Jay rose to greet him and asked, "Can I get you something?"

"No, thanks."

As they walked out to the cab, Jay said, "Let's try the Chevrolet dealer first."

When they arrived at the lot, he jumped out and began inspecting the used pickups. By the time a salesperson showed up, he had selected one he wanted to drive. It had everything he wanted, including a tool chest bolted to the pickup bed. It was almost too good to be true. He drove it several blocks and decided it was what he needed. The deal was completed and the salesperson handed him the keys.

"Ben, will you go ahead and let me follow you back to the motel in my pickup?"

"Yes, glad to."

"Along the way, would you stop somewhere, so I can buy some work clothes and boots?"

"Sure. If you don't mind, how about if I stop by in the morning and guide you to where there are several stores, so you'll have a choice?"

"Okay."

"Then follow me and you'll soon be back at the Sipes Motel."

They arrived shortly. "Thanks," Jay called, and waved as Ben left. He parked, got out, and walked away, feeling pleased with his purchase.

Despite his losses, he was in better shape, financially, than others he knew, thanks to his friend's advice to "Put a few dollars in a bank in your home country." He wished he had doubled the amount and sent more while he had it, but there was no use brooding over what he should have done.

To tell the truth, he had no complaint. Nevertheless, there were moments when he missed Antonita terribly. Yet, he still believed he had made the right decision to return to the States and find a job. Things had a way of working out for him. They had before, during his frustrating days searching for Susan Johnson in England. Eventually, he realized it was not meant for him to find her.

Putting aside the past for now, he whistled a cheery tune and sauntered into the motel office with his hands in his pockets.

Ned Sipes said, "You must've had a good day."

"Yes," Jay replied, with a wide grin on his face. Dragging something from his pocket, he said, "These are the keys to my pickup."

"Yeah. I saw it when you parked."

As the two chatted, an attractive young lady entered the lobby.

"Jay, this is our daughter, Sue Ann. She just returned from visiting our relatives back East. We're really proud of her. She made the Dean's List at college both semesters and still managed to help out at the motel."

"Congratulations!" said Jay. "Was this your first year of college?"

"No, my second. I'm majoring in elementary education. But enough about me. Dad says you're a civil engineer, and you grew up in South America and speak perfect Spanish."

"Since Spanish was the language I heard everywhere I went, I learned it well. As a result of growing up in those countries, I speak better Spanish than I do English."

"You must have had some fascinating experiences living and working there. We would like to have you share them with us while you're here," said Sue Ann.

"I will," Jay said, smiling. "Now that I have my pickup, we could go to the ice cream parlor or a movie, if you like."

"I would prefer to get some ice cream, so we can talk," said Sue Ann.

"Of course, you'll have to guide me there," Jay teased.

"No problem," she replied. "I've lived here all my life."

"Good. How about tomorrow night?"

"Yes, if you promise to tell me something about where you lived in those countries. Dad said you mentioned a ranch located a long distance from town."

"It was quite an experience, Sue Ann, living in the most primitive area between Peru and Bolivia. I'll be glad to tell you what it was like in those days, when what we didn't produce on the ranch, we had to order several months ahead and have it brought in by pack mules."

They talked a few minutes longer, then Jay said, "I've enjoyed talking with you. Will I see you at dinner tonight?"

Sue Ann grinned and said, "Yes, I'll be serving the food."

Jay left and went to his room. It had been a long day and he needed to unwind before going to sample Grace Sipes' down-home cooking.

Leaning back in the easy chair, he reflected on how God had blessed him that day. He had helped him get the pickup he'd been looking for, and he got to meet the Sipes' lovely daughter. Jay smiled to himself; if a little trust in God produced all this, maybe he needed a lot more of it.

He picked up the driver's manual and began skimming it. When the hour came to go to dinner, he had already covered over half the book. It looked easy enough and he decided that if he could find the State Patrol Office, he would apply for his license the next day. If something happened and he failed the first time, he could try again. He put the book aside and went to dinner.

Soon after he sat down, Sue Ann came over to take his order and said, "I haven't eaten, Jay. Would you mind if I joined you for dinner?"

"Not at all," Jay said, smiling. "I'd be delighted."

She returned shortly, carrying a large tray with their food and sat across from him.

"I'm honored," said Jay.

"So am I," Sue Ann told him. "This is my first chance to meet someone who has grown up in South America. It gives me an opportunity to practice my Spanish with a pro."

"Don't forget, Sue Ann, it's a romantic language," Jay said, grinning.

"Muy romantico, yes?" Sue Ann asked.

"Right!" Jay said. "I can see you'll have no problem with the language. Earlier you said you wanted to hear about life on the ranch. Well, we had an Indian village of fifty families who were descendants of the ancient Inca who once ruled most of South America. One of our borders was an old stone road built by the Inca when they were in power. These stone roads helped Inca rulers communicate with their subjects in the various countries.

"Since we were located in a lovely, picturesque setting, many people came to visit. Teachers from the mission school I attended sometimes spent their vacations in our home. When one teacher's turn came, I went with my parents to meet her at the river crossing over to our house. Though everyone spoke Spanish at school, one day I overheard her tell another in English that I was a trouble maker. She blamed me for all that went wrong in our second grade class room. Consequently, I disliked her and didn't want to be around during her visit.

"The next morning, I told my mother that I was going to spend those two weeks with friends in the Indian village. I saddled my pony, Cayuse, and took along some feed and my sleeping bag. As I told her good-by, I said, 'Let me know when she leaves and I'll come home.' To inform my parents that I'd arrived safely, I wrote a nice letter to them in English and sent it by way of a man from the village who worked for Dad.

"At the end of two weeks, Mother sent word that the teacher had left and I went home. She later told me that when she showed my letter to this teacher, she'd said, 'I didn't know that kid knew how to speak English.'

"Then I explained to Mother what she had told the other teacher about me. Mother asked, 'Jay, what did you learn from that experience?'

'Not to say bad things about people in any language.'"

"Was it far to your school?" Sue Ann asked.

"It was the same distance from the ranch as it was to town. Two days on horseback to get there. I boarded at the mission school. I was a lonely little boy until I made friends with kids my age."

"Jay, you've had some interesting experiences. I'm looking forward to tomorrow night."

"So am I, Sue Ann. The dinner was super and I enjoyed every bite. I've gotta go finish reading the driver's manual before bedtime. I must get my license and write my résumés to send out for job interviews."

"It shouldn't be too tough to get your license," said Sue Ann.

"I don't know. Never can tell," Jay said, sighing.

"If you don't make it this first time, you can try again."

"That's encouraging. Good night, Sue Ann."

Back in his room, Jay read the manual and thought, with my experience, I can pass this test. In South American countries, I drove anything with a motor and four wheels over all kinds of terrain, even heavy, road-building equipment used for construction. He remembered Ben saying, "You shouldn't have trouble getting a license," and put aside the manual and went to bed.

After breakfast the following morning, he asked Ned Sipes for directions to the State Patrol Office and left to apply for his driver's license. The route Ned suggested was nothing like the one Ben had led him through the previous day. He ended up on the opposite side of the city and had to ask a policeman for directions. Eventually, he got on a street he recognized and drove right to the State Patrol Office. As a car pulled out, he parked in the empty spot and hurried inside. The place was full. He would need to wait.

At last his turn came. After he completed the written part he had to wait for the test drive. Eventually, an instructor came over and said, "If you're ready, you can go for your driving test."

"I'm ready," said Jay. He walked out and got into his pickup on the driver's side.

The instructor followed and asked, "Is everything clear regarding this test?"

"Yes," Jay said and the pickup jumped forward. He followed the instructor's directions as to which way to turn and what street to take next. Jay relaxed and made occasional comments during the drive. After the test was over, he felt confident of he'd passed. He followed the instructor back inside and sat down to wait for his temporary license.

A few minutes later, his instructor came over and said, "Mr. Ryan, I'm sorry we can't issue your license today. You failed the driving test."

Unsure he had understood, Jay asked, "Did you say I failed the driving test?"

"Yes."

"How could I? I followed all your instructions."

"Not entirely. You were too casual and talked with the instructor."

"I need that license. I must have it in order to get a job," Jay said.

"Then study the manual. When you feel you're ready for the test, come back to see us."

"Of all the rotten luck. I can't believe it," Jay muttered, while walking out to his pickup. "I have an international driver's license accepted anywhere in South America, and I fail the test in my own country. Enrique would not believe it. I'll have to review the manual and try again."

After sitting and reflecting on what had happened, he decided it was too early to return to the motel. He needed a change of scene. Shopping for work clothes appealed to him, even if he had failed the test and had no job.

It was after two o'clock when he finished his shopping and found a place to get a bowl of soup and a sandwich. Later in his motel room, he looked at what he had bought. It was everything he needed, once he got a job. Surely he could work something out. He sat down and studied the driving manual again until dinner.

When he went to eat, Sue Ann was nowhere in sight. Had she changed her mind about going with him to the ice cream parlor? He asked Ned about her.

"Our regular cleaning girl left at noon to attend her brother's wedding. Sue Ann had to finish the cleaning after she got home from school. She said tell you to go ahead and eat. She'll be in later."

"Good. I was getting worried," said Jay.

A few minutes afterward, Sue Ann entered the room. Her curls were still damp from her shower.

"Sorry I'm late, Jay."

"I'm glad you're here," he said. "Can you imagine me trying to find the ice cream parlor alone, no better than I know Los Angeles?"

"If you'll excuse me, I'll get our trays."

"Let me help," said Jay.

Back at the table, Sue Ann asked, "How did the test go?"

"Would you believe I flunked it, Sue Ann? After my experiences driving in South America, the test was so easy, I felt confident of passing. Then I made a few remarks to the instructor while he was giving it. As a result, no license."

"Don't worry, Jay. Next time you'll pass."

"I hope so. Sure deflated my ego, but I'll forget it for tonight. How was your day?"

"Busy as usual, rushing from one class to the next. I'll be glad when I graduate and go on to teach."

"You remind me of myself when I was in engineering school in Chile. I couldn't wait to earn my degree and go to work."

"Yet you hung in there and graduated, didn't you?" asked Sue Ann.

"Yes. Letting my parents know I'd graduated was a highlight of my life."

"Excuse me, Jay. Can we leave now for the ice cream parlor?"

"Yeah, let's go. You don't mind driving my pickup, do you?"

"Not if you trust me."

Along the way she shared a bit of history about that part of town. At the ice cream parlor she said, "Let's sit at this small table in the corner, away from the crowd."

While they ate, Sue Ann asked, "Jay, how have you managed to stay single? In all those interesting places you must have met some attractive young women. Did none of them take your heart?"

"I lost a chance to marry my childhood sweetheart, an English nurse, who also grew up in South America. She disappeared in England during the war and I was never able to find her. A few years later, when I had vowed I was not going to fall in love again, I met an elegant, young woman who took my heart. She was from a wealthy and prominent family, but after I lost everything in the takeover, there was nothing to offer her. I didn't want us to marry and be supported by her family. So I came back to the States. From what I've shared, you can see how circumstances really changed my life."

"You miss her don't you?"

"Terribly, but I did what I believed was the best thing for both of us. After I faced the facts, I came to realize she would never have been happy with me. What about you? You're an attractive young lady, Sue Ann."

"Thanks. To be truthful, between my work and college, I have little free time. I hope to graduate in three years and begin teaching."

"I admire your discipline. You know what you want and you're working toward achieving your goal."

They chatted a while longer, then Sue Ann said, "Jay, I could listen to you talk all night, but I should get back and study for my eight A.M. test in psychology."

"You're the driver," Jay said, smiling.

Back at the motel, he said, "Thanks a million, Sue Ann, for a lovely evening."

She asked, "Did the ice cream parlor remind you of South America?"

"Yes. It brought to mind the happiest years of my life with my parents on the ranch. We liked ice cream, but the only way we could have it was to make our own. It was my job to turn the hand-cranked freezer until the mixture froze. This process took such a long while I thought it would never happen."

"I'm curious, where did you get the ice?"

"During the week we saved ice cubes from our kerosene-operated refrigerator until there was enough to make two gallons of ice cream. This was something I looked forward to each Saturday afternoon."

"Think you'll return in the future?"

"Yes, if God wills," said Jay.

# CHAPTER THREE

In the quietness before he fell asleep, Jay reviewed the pleasant evening he had spent with Sue Ann. What a perceptive young woman. Like him, she knew what she wanted to become at an early age. Working to reach goals she had set for herself was admirable. Listening to her talk about the future and when she was teaching, she sounded so positive.

He admired her self-discipline, perhaps no easy task for a strong-willed young lady. She reminded him of Susan. He decided the two would have had much in common. Then he thought of the differences between Sue Ann and Antonita. Upon telling Antonita, "I've lost everything, I'm broke," she'd said, "No problem. After our wedding, we can live with my parents." He chuckled thinking about what Sue Ann's comment would be under similar circumstances. She helped her parents make a success of their motel, while taking a full load of classes in college. She was independent and looked forward to graduating and being out on her own. He could not imagine Sue Ann telling her future husband, "If you don't have a job, we can move in with Mom and Dad."

Then he reminded himself that Antonita and Sue Ann had been raised in two different cultures, which greatly affected how they acted or reacted. Regardless, during the moments when he was alone, he thought about Antonita. She knew how to bring out the best in people. No wonder he had adored her. The night he walked out of her life, it had taken all his will power to keep going and not turn back.

He was grateful for time spent with the Sipes family. What a blessing they had been to him. The evening helped him realize he had made a wise decision to return to his country. He had determined his own destiny. By setting goals and working toward them, perhaps he would attain the desired results. Writing an eye-catching résumé to attract attention and help him get job interviews was his first priority. Retaking the test for his California driver's license was next. Believing he was pursuing the right course, he thanked God for guidance and went to sleep.

The next morning, he awoke early, refreshed by the night's rest. After showering and dressing, he sat down and wrote his long-term goals. He glanced at the list and saw he had given top priority to landing a good job, saving his money, and returning to South America.

When he went to breakfast, Ned Sipes said, "Jay, there's a guest here from San Francisco. He told me his company is advertising for an experienced civil engineer. I thought I'd pass the word on to you in case you're interested."

"Thanks for thinking of me, Ned . This may be worth checking into. I'd like to meet him and see what his company has in mind." Jay ordered breakfast and was waiting to be served when the guest entered.

After a few minutes, Ned and the guest came over. "Jay, this is Larry Williams."

"I'm Jay Ryan, glad to meet you," said Jay, rising and shaking hands with him. "How about joining me for breakfast?"

"Thanks, I will," said Larry, sitting down.

They chatted until Mrs. Sipes brought their food. Jay learned that Larry's company, Miller and Sons, General Contractors, was interested in submitting a bid to improve Highway One. Since the state had received no bids by the due date, they were encouraging a bid from his company.

"Have you had experience in rock work and retaining walls in sheered cliffs over two thousand feet from the ocean bed?" Larry asked.

"Yes, I did that kind of work in South America."

"Then you may be the engineer the company needs. Here's my business card. If you're interesteded, submit your résumé to this address."

"Thanks, Larry. I'll get it to them this week. It sure sounds challenging."

"Without a doubt, it will be. Sorry, I've gotta run. It's been a pleasure talking with you and I hope to see you again."

Back in his room, Jay decided that getting his driver's license was first on the agenda. Once he did, he would be free to work on other things. Suddenly he remembered he needed to prepare his résumé for Miller and Sons. Reluctantly, he put aside studying for his driver's test and spent the day writing and rewriting his résumé. After making numerous mistakes with his phonetic spelling of English words, he selected the best one of the lot.

After breakfast the next morning, he searched for a typist. It was not easy to find one, but around noon he found an office with a public stenographer who agreed to do the work. Realizing that a Spanish-English dictionary could be helpful, Jay went to a bookstore across the street and bought one.

He was hoping to talk with Larry Williams again, but upon reaching the motel he learned that Larry had already checked out. No matter, he would just send off his application and résumé.

Determined to try for the driver's test, Jay got into his pickup and drove to the State Patrol Office. Once inside, he looked around, but didn't see his instructor from the other day. He strode over to another man and told him, "My name's Jay Ryan and I'm here to take my driving test."

"Very well, Mr. Ryan. If you're ready, let's go," said the instructor.

They walked out and got into Jay's pickup.

Jay kept quiet and followed the instructions. When they returned to the office, he went inside and sat down. It appeared no one was in a hurry. His palms felt sweaty and he wondered what went wrong this time.

He began making plans to try again when the instructor came over and said, "Sorry you had to wait Mr. Ryan. Here's your temporary license."

"Thanks, I was getting concerned. Afraid I'd failed again," Jay said.

"You passed with no problem."

Jay looked at the license and marveled at what a difference it had made in his life. Success at last. While whistling a merry tune, he headed for the motel to share his news. When he stepped inside, Sue Ann was working in the front office.

Observing the happy expression on his face, she asked, "What happened?"

"I made it. I passed my driving test!"

"I knew you would."

"Can you get away long enough to go to the ice cream parlor? This occasion calls for a celebration with a super banana split."

"Let me call Dad and see if he'll take over."

When Ned came in from doing yard work, he said, "I'll keep shop if you promise to bring one home to me."

"Sure, Ned."

At the ice cream parlor, Jay said, "I'm glad you agreed to come with me. It's a double pleasure sharing one's good news with friends. How was your day?"

"Different. I met the most interesting guy, a new student in my psychology class. He also plans to teach when he graduates."

"Sounds exciting, Sue Ann. Think he'll be "Mister Right"?"

"I don't know. He has goals and long-range plans, same as I have. And like me, he has to dash from one class to the next, so there's little time for us to talk to each other."

"Sue Ann, you have to make time."

"Yes, I suppose so," she replied.

They lingered a few minutes longer at the ice cream parlor, then Jay said, "I know you probably want to get back to your studies."

"Sometimes my self-discipline gets worrisome, like a hard taskmaster is standing over me. Then I remind myself that I set the goals."

"I'll see if Ned's banana split is ready to travel and we'll leave," Jay said.

"Glad you remembered. If we'd shown up without it, he would have sent us back."

As they left, Sue Ann selected a scenic drive to the motel. When she gave Ned the masterpiece of banana splits, she said, "Enjoy it, Dad."

"Thanks, I will," he said, quickly digging into the showy confection.

A week after Jay mailed his résumé to the company in San Francisco, he received a letter stating they would pay for his expenses if he came for an interview. He answered their letter that day, saying he was interested and could be there the following Monday, if that was satisfactory.

He worked to get things in order for the trip. Since he would be driving his pickup, he had it checked to avoid the possibility of a mechanical problem. He didn't want to get stranded somewhere along the road and run the risk of missing the interview.

Meanwhile, he studied the daily newspapers looking for local job opportunities in the event he wasn't hired. An ad for an opening near Grand Junction caught his attention. It was strange, he had not thought of that place since he had been a patient there after the war. He wrote a letter and included a copy of his résumé. Before he mailed it, the company in San Francisco sent a second letter stating they were waiting for his arrival.

After he got to bed, he remembered that, in his haste to get his driver's license and a pickup, he had not contacted

Grandad Bill. Hopping out of bed, he wrote him a long letter saying he was in the States and was going for an interview with a company in San Francisco. He promised to keep in touch and let him know if he got the job. He closed his letter with: "Grandad, write to me in care of the Sipes Motel in Los Angeles. They'll forward your letter to me. Love, your grandson, Jay."

As he planned to leave early Friday morning, he told Ned Sipes, "Please get my bill ready. I've enjoyed staying here, and to show my appreciation for your thoughtfulness and kindness to me, I want to take the three of you to dinner on Thursday evening. You are more familiar with the local restaurants, so you choose where we'll go."

"You don't need to do that, Jay," Ned protested.

"I know," said Jay, "but I want to."

"Very well, we'll be happy to go," Ned replied.

When Thursday night came, Ned told Jay, "We'll go in our car and leave your pickup for the long haul tomorrow."

Jay couldn't believe it when he came to the front office and saw how elegant they looked. As he helped Sue Ann into the back seat, she asked, "Jay, does this make you think of South America?"

He smiled and said, "Yes. Reminds me of nights when I was escorting a lovely young lady, like you, to the movies or dinner. Why do you ask?"

"You seem happier than when you first came," she said.

"I am. You don't know what a treasure the three of you are and how you've helped me get my life in order."

"Thanks, Jay," Ned told him.

"I think you'll like where we're going tonight. It's near the college," said Sue Ann.

Before long, Ned turned down a quiet street and parked in front of a restaurant.

"This is the place I was telling you about," said Sue Ann as they entered.

A part of the city Jay had not seen, he liked the quiet, relaxed atmosphere. A trio played beautiful Spanish music while they dined.

Grace asked, "Like in South America?"

"Yes," Jay said, smiling.

"One of our favorite places we thought you'd like," said Sue Ann.

"I do. It's marvelous and the food is special."

After a pleasant evening, Jay said good night, returned to the motel, and went to his room. As he got into bed, he reviewed the events of the day and realized he would miss these gracious friends and owners of the Sipes Motel.

At breakfast the next morning, Sue Ann and Grace brought the lunch they had packed for him.

"We hope you like it," said Sue Ann.

"I'm sure I will. How can I thank you?" Jay asked.

"You might try giving us each a hug," said Sue Ann, grinning.

"My pleasure," Jay said, rising and hugging first Sue Ann, then Grace.

"Have a safe trip," said Sue Ann. "I've gotta run to my first class."

"Speaking of running, I must leave," Jay said, glancing at his watch. "Good luck in your studies and take care, Sue Ann." Thanking them for the lunch, he climbed into his pickup and headed for San Francisco.

Excited at the prospect of this interview leading to a job, he sped along listening to the steady hum of the pickup's motor. He decided it had been worth the money and relaxed. Feeling like a new person, and with the road virtually to himself, he was really putting the miles behind him, when out of nowhere a patrolman pulled him over.

"What's wrong, Officer?"

"Didn't you see the speed limit sign as you reached town? You should only be going twenty-five miles per hour."

"No, sir. I saw a sign near the road, but it must have been turned around. There was nothing written on it."

"Hmph, if it's knocked down, that's the third time this month. I won't ticket you today, but watch your speed."

"Thanks, Officer, I will."

As he drove on, he reproached himself for not staying alert and watching his speed. A few miles farther, fog began to roll in, making it hard to see what the surrounding countryside looked like.

Driving at the legal speed with his lights on, he was surprised when a station wagon crept up behind him and followed for miles along the narrow, winding road. He realized the driver's intention was to pass him, despite the poor visibility. Fearing a collision, he pulled over to the side. The driver honked his horn as he zoomed past and met a car speeding toward him from the opposite direction. The two vehicles hit head on. The force of the impact spun both cars around and around until they finally came to a stop. Now they were blocking the highway, so no other traffic could get beyond the scene of the accident.

Smoke poured from under the hood of the station wagon. Jay ran over and found steam escaping from a broken water hose. The driver was slumped over the steering wheel. The front end of the smaller car had been smashed, making it impossible to free the driver. The woman was either dead or unconscious, but the man beside her appeared to be alive.

Jay got some flares from his pickup and set them out to warn approaching traffic that the road wasn't clear. Soon the lights of other cars shone through the fog on both sides of the highway. Someone reported the accident to the State Patrol. Another called for an ambulance and a wrecker. The three arrived at the scene shortly.

The wrecker worked to pry the vehicles apart in order to free the couple in the small car. The ambulance then transported the injured to a nearby hospital. An hour later, the road was finally cleared and traffic began moving again.

As Jay got into his pickup, the investigating patrolman said, "Keep in touch with us, Mr. Ryan. Since you saw the accident, you may be called as a witness in the event of a law suit."

"Very well," Jay said.

As he continued his journey to San Francisco, he thought about how quickly circumstances can change. Had the first patrolman not advised him to slow down and take it easy, or had he failed to pull off the road to let the station wagon pass him, his name might have been on the list of those injured or killed.

By the time he reached San Jose, the fog had lifted, and he began to enjoy the drive. He drove faster hoping to reach San Francisco before dark, but it was dusk when he arrived. When he pulled into a gas station, he asked the attendant about a place to stay for the weekend.

"There's a small, family-owned and operated hotel about ten blocks down the street. You can't miss it, " he said.

Following his directions, Jay arrived and parked out front. Going inside, he told the desk clerk, "Hope you have a room for me. I've driven all the way from L.A. and I'm tired."

"Register and then I'll show you to your room. The dining area is open if you care to eat."

"I'm not hungry, but I would like a tall glass of milk sent to my room."

"Will do, Mr. Ryan. Come along and I'll take you to room 203. This your first visit to San Francisco?"

"Yes."

"Then you'll probably enjoy the view of the city from your window."

As soon as Jay drank the glass of milk, he undressed and got into bed. He fell asleep at once and did not wake up until eight A.M. As soon as he had showered and dressed, he hurried down to a breakfast of fresh fruit.

After talking with the owners at length and asking countless questions about the city, he left in his pickup and spent the day exploring. By late afternoon, he had driven on most of the streets that were not too steep. He stopped by the park and observed families with children. He had even located the company's office and found the shortest route to it from the hotel. Pleased with what he had learned, he returned to the hotel before dark. After supper, he talked with the owners some more and learned that their parents came from India.

He spent a quiet day on Sunday resting, seeking God's guidance for his life, and writing a letter to his friend Enrique. He enclosed a picture post card of historic San Francisco. Then he sent a card to the Sipes that showed where he ate lunch on Sunday.

On Monday morning, he rose early, ate breakfast, and left. He had no way of knowing what he might see as he drove along. The city was interesting and different. There were people from countries all over the world. He noticed some groups still clung to their old world customs and way of living.

When he arrived for the interview, Brick Todd welcomed him and said, "Glad you made it. I'll give you a quick rundown on what we're planning. The state is calling for a second round of bids for improving Highway One. The State Highway Department is encouraging us to submit a bid.

"After reading your résumé and seeing the experience you've had in rock work, you may be the engineer we need for this project . However, there's a problem. You have no work references from the United States, so we would have to hire you on probation."

"I understand and I accept your offer. I need to gain some experience working here in the States and obtain references for future jobs."

While they talked the general manager, Terrance Rutherford, entered and asked, "Have you decided anything?"

"Yes, I believe he's the engineer for the project, but he'll need to spend a few days in the office for orientation."

"Can you leave for the project after you've gone through orientation?" Terrance asked.

"Yes," Jay said, then added, "I should tell you that on my way to San Francisco, I was the first one on the scene of a car accident in which a person was killed. I may get a notice to appear in court as a witness."

"We'll face that problem if it appears," said the chief engineer. "In the meantime, while you're here you should sign these papers. We'll get a copy of the specifications for the bid, so you can study them. I'll also set up a visit to the site."

Everything was going great with his work in the office, so Jay forgot all about the car accident until he received a summons to testify in court in two days. When he showed it to the chief engineer, he said, "I'll postpone the trip until you return."

"Hope this won't cause a problem for the company," said Jay.

"I'm sure it won't. Check with me when you're back in town."

"Thanks, I sure appreciate this consideration."

Jay drove to the town near the scene of the accident. After he told his version of what happened and was questioned, he was released and allowed to report to his job.

When he returned, the chief engineer said, "We'll visit the project tomorrow."

The next morning, they left for the site.

"Wow!" Jay exclaimed upon seeing it. "If I didn't know I was in the United States, I'd believe I was in the South American Andes Mountains. I can see how this road, built during the era when there was no heavy earth-moving equipment, presented challenges to the engineers and others working on it."

"Yeah," the chief said, "and a few may have lost their lives if they traveled near the road's edge and tumbled over the cliffs to the depths below."

"It offers the traveler a fantastic view from these heights," Jay said, glancing at the Pacific Ocean a few thousand feet below them. He saw a car move to one side of the narrow road, making room for a large produce truck going the other way.

Two days later, Jay and his helper, a knowledgeable person, left for the project. They worked every day from seven

A.M. until five P.M. for two weeks, gathering information Jay needed for working on the company's project bid.

A few weeks before the bid opening, there was an ad in the newspaper saying this road project had been postponed indefinitely. Brick Todd left to confer with the State Highway Department to learn what caused the change in their plans. They advised him to wait until they activated the project. He gave Jay the bad news the morning after he returned.

Jay said to Brick, "I'll begin looking for another job."

Then Terrance Rutherford told him, "The company has several things you can advise on while we're waiting for the state's decision. We'll retain you in the office."

Months passed with no news from the state.

Brick said, "Our company has contracted to replace a bridge. One of the piers has been undermined. It lost its alignment and has buckled the bridge's steel structure. We need an engineer to look at it and make some recommendations. Have you had experience in such situations, Jay?"

"Yes," Jay said.

"In order to understand our options, we'll send an engineer to the area. After he spends a few days gathering infomation, he can advise us. Are you interested?"

"Yes, where's it located?"

"In Arizona, three miles north of Flagstaff. It's no problem for us as we're general contractors registered to do any kind of work in the four neighboring states. Our main office, located in Los Angeles, is handling this contract. Check with them."

"I'll leave for Los Angeles tomorrow," said Jay.

# CHAPTER FOUR

When Jay returned to the hotel, he called Ned Sipes in Los Angeles and said, "I'll be there tomorrow night. Please save a room for me."

"Your room's ready, Jay. See you when you get here."

The next morning, he left San Francisco at sunrise. During this trip the weather cooperated and he enjoyed the scenery. He wished to linger and view the countryside from the Golden Gate bridge, but he had to get to L.A. Driving through vineyard country reminded him of the tasty homemade jams and jellies Nell Sipes served at breakfast. At the first fruit stand he reached, he bought them a gift basket of grapes.

It was eight P.M. when he parked in front of the Sipes Motel and went inside.

"If you're hungry, Grace has beans with hamhock, corn bread, peach cobbler, and all kinds of good things," said Ned.

"That sounds great," Jay said.

While he ate, he filled the family in on what had happened since he left.

"I'll be going to bed as soon as I finish eating. Tomorrow I have to check in with the same company about a job in a different location."

Before he went to his room, he remembered the grapes in his pickup.

"Excuse me, while I get a little something for you out of my truck."

When he returned and set his gift on the table, the family was delighted.

Grace said, "Thanks for thinking of us."

Jay smiled and said,"My pleasure and thank you, Grace, for the tasty food. I hope you never lose your cooking skills." He said good night and left.

Later, after he got into bed, he lay awake reflecting on his losses as a result of the takeover and not getting reimbursed. He had worked hard for what he earned. It had not come easy. Now that he was out of the country, what happened seemed unreal. Questions flashed through his mind like streaks of lightning he had seen high in the Andes Mountains.

Along the way, he had hired poor people who were eager to work and wanted to improve the quality of their lives. He recalled how some contractors had expressed envy at how he had no difficulty finding and keeping adequate help and they asked him for his secret.

"Simple," he said. "I tell workers what I want them to do and how to do it. Then I pay them well and see that they have good food every day they're on the job."

He wept as he remembered how the takeover had affected the Indian population. In certain sections of the country, some groups banded together and killed people, burning their houses and taking their land, just like they had taken his jungle property. However, what these groups did worsened their situation. They lacked the economical resources they hoped to gain from every takeover to improve their lot in life.

What joy and satisfaction he felt remembering the small good deeds he had done for several Indian communities who lived near the roads he was building. At no cost to them, he made a road or leveled a soccer field in their small villages. To show their appreciation, one village prepared a feast. He could not believe the work it took to dig a large pit that was eighteen feet in diameter. They let a fire burn in the pit a day and a night, removed the unburned material, then put on a layer of banana leaves. On top of that they placed raw ribs and legs of pigs, goats, and lambs. This was covered with banana leaves and a layer of hot rocks from around the circle of fire. The next section contained a layer of chickens, turkeys, and guinea pigs covered with banana leaves and hot rocks. Unhusked corn, yucca, potatoes, and other produce became the last layer, covered with banana leaves and more hot rocks. The entire pyramid (called pachamanka) was then covered with ten inches of dirt that had been dug up to make the pit. A day and a night later, they opened the pachamanka and feasted on the tastiest food Jay had ever eaten.

Before he fell asleep, he thought of Antonita and wondered had she really cared as much for him as she indicated? Time would tell. Resolutely, he put thoughts of her aside and went to sleep.

At nine A.M. the next day he drove to Miller and Sons' main office. Upon his arrival, he met with John Brownell, assistant engineer.

"We've been expecting you, Jay."

He spent the day in conference with John going over the information the company had on the bridge project.

"How far is it from L.A.?" Jay asked.

"Two days travel. The last day will be over rutted dirt and gravel roads. It's urgent you get there soon and make a visual survey of the situation. Gather enough facts to help us decide what we should do. Can you leave in the morning?"

"Yes," Jay replied.

"Good! Come by the office and pick up Slim Eastman. He knows the way to camp and will be your helper on the survey."

"Thanks. I'll be here," Jay said. En route to the motel, he looked foward to a good meal and getting a night's rest.

It was eight A.M. the next day when Jay and Slim left the Los Angeles office. Bright sunshine lifted Jay's spirits and he asked, "Isn't it great to have nice weather?"

"Yeah," said Slim, "it's more cheerful when the sun shines."

They headed for Kingman, located about halfway to camp. They stopped only for gas and food. It was almost dark when they arrived and found a motel to spend the night. Before Jay fell asleep, he thought, it's strange how weary I was when I got here. I've always enjoyed the scenery while driving to a new job and looked forward to facing the challenges it affords. It's different this time. At the rate I'm going, by the time I reach camp I'll be unable to do my best work.

As soon as they ate breakfast and left the following morning, Jay told Slim, "I hope our luck holds and we reach camp today."

"We should," said Slim, "but you're gonna find the road to camp something else."

"They said it was ruts, dirt, and gravel."

"They told you right," Slim said. "I've never seen a worse strip to drive on." When they reached this section, Jay sighed and said, "I feel sorry for my pickup."

They bounced along for two hours with Jay struggling to find the smoothest side of the road. Then it grew dark. The wind blew and rain poured, making it impossible to see ahead, despite the windshield wipers swishing across at top speed.

"If this keeps up, Slim, we'll get stranded."

"Yeah, or drowned. Look how the water's rolling down the hillsides."

"Wow! Look what's ahead of us," said Jay, stopping a few feet back from a torrent of muddy water.

"Hey, there's the remains of an old buggy and some cows that didn't make it," said Slim.

As they waited for the water to get low enough for a safe crossing, Jay said, "It would sure help, if they'd put in a few culverts to take care of this heavy run-off."

"Well, Jay, they don't need 'em 'til there's a cloudburst like this."

An hour later, the water receded. Slim said, "If we're careful, we can make it."

"I'm hungry," said Jay. "Wish I'd thought to have the motel pack a lunch for us."

"We're not far from a service station with a lunchroom," said Slim.

"Good. I'll be ready for it."

When they arrived, Jay drove past the pump, switched off the motor, and they ran inside.

"What'll it be?" asked the man behind the counter. "Today's special is hot bean soup, burgers, and coffee."

"I'll take the special," Jay told him.

"Make mine the same," said Slim.

"Looks like the rain's 'bout to quit," said the man.

By the time they finished their meal, the sky had cleared. It was as if the cloudburst had only been a light shower.

As they left, Jay asked, "Think we'll make camp before dark?"

Slim looked out and said, "Dunno. Even if you've been raised here, you can't tell about the weather or how much water a cloudburst has left in these dry creek beds."

"Yeah. It makes them dangerous to cross over. Like I said earlier, Slim, it would help, if they'd put in some culverts to take care of the run-off."

"Guess so, but it would cost money and not many folks live in this area."

Hours later and lurching from side to side to stay in the ruts, Slim yelled, "I see the camp lights!"

"Best news I've heard all day. How far is it?"

"Four or five miles."

"The closer the better. I'm ready to eat and get to bed," said Jay.

When they arrived, Jay said, "What a drive. I'd hate to make it often." He parked by the main building as Max Provo, camp superintendent, ran out.

"Am I glad to see you two! I've been waiting and watching since six P.M."

"Without Slim as copilot, I'd still be wandering in the mountains," Jay confessed.

"Are you hungry?" asked Max.

"Yes," both replied.

"Then come in and grab your plates before the cook closes the kitchen. When you finish eating, I'll show you where you're gonna sleep while you're here."

That night, Jay slept soundly. After a tasty breakfast prepared by the camp cook, he and Max left to walk the bridge site. Jay took several pictures and told Max he would start the survey the next morning.

He found the project challenging. Being outdoors and working with nature gave him new life at first. Then as the hours passed, he began to feel tired. By the end of the second week, he found it difficult to get through the day. The necessary walking he had to do taxed his endurance to the limit. Pain in his side and legs was becoming unbearable. He wondered what was going on inside his body. He finished the survey and returned to the main office with the information.

While discussing his findings with the chief engineer, C. J. Berry, the following day, they were interrupted by the receptionist who delivered a note to C. J.

He read it, then said, "The damaged pier has collasped and the bridge is in the water. Get back there and see what should be done."

"Yes, sir," Jay said and left for camp. He regretted not having a chance to tell him about his health problem. It looked as if there was no way out. He would have to endure the pain and finish the job.

Back at the project, Jay could not believe what he was seeing. The bridge was in the water as a result of the damaged pier giving way. He radioed C. J. and advised, "Cut the steel structure into pieces and haul it to a waste or storage site. Then blast the fallen concrete pier and clean out the hole so another pier can be built in the future."

"Go ahead and get started," ordered C. J.

The necessary equipment was brought in and the task of dismantling the fallen bridge began. Jay hoped to finish the project in a few weeks, so he could leave to seek the medical help he needed. Unfortunately, it did not happen. As soon as one problem was solved, another tough one loomed before them. Much as he wanted to stay with the job, he knew he could not do so. Intense pain in his side and legs kept him awake nights and hindered him from doing the work.

He radioed C. J. again and said, "Please send someone to take over my job. I'm sick and leaving for a veteran's hospital." He said farewell to the crew at the job site, tucked his belongings in the tool chest, and left that morning.

Hours dragged on and the pain in his side worsened. "Dear God," he prayed, help me get to a hospital." He drove through three towns before he finally found one. At the emergency room desk, he said, "I'm a war veteran passing through on my way to the veterans hospital in Grand Junction. I need to see a doctor and have something prescribed for the pain."

After the doctor talked with Jay and examined him, he said, "It sounds like the pain is internal. The hospital where you're going will have the facilities to take care of your problem. We'll give you something to help you sleep tonight. If you feel up to traveling tomorrow, it would be wise to drive on to Grand Junction."

Soon afterward, a nurse gave him the medication and he slept soundly. When the doctor made his rounds in the morning, Jay was already dressed and ready to leave as soon as he paid his bill.

"Can you make it?" asked the doctor.

"I think so," Jay replied. "I feel better after getting a good night's sleep."

Jay felt fine the first few hours of driving, but in the afternoon, the hours dragged on and the pain in his side grew worse. As he wondered how much farther he had to drive, he saw the hospital. He stopped his pickup and turned off the ignition before he blacked out.

The guard at the gate saw his slumped figure draped over the steering wheel and called for help. Jay came to while being wheeled to emergency.

The doctor on duty asked, "What seems to be the problem? Where do you hurt?"

"My side and legs," Jay gasped.

"Obviously you suffered severe wounds in the war. To what stateside hospital were you sent when you were wounded?"

"San Diego. This is the second time I've been admitted to this hospital. I was flown here in critical condition from the main hospital. I was a patient for over five months and underwent several operations and therapy. When I recovered and was discharged from the hospital, I requested the U.S. Air Force fly me back to Chile. That was where I volunteered for the American Air Force in Santiago."

"We'll get you to a room and give you something to ease the pain," said the doctor.

"Thanks, I'd appreciate it," Jay said.

The next day, Dr. Ted Owen came to his room with two other surgeons.

"Jay," Dr. Owen began, "according to your medical records, you had severe internal injuries when you were wounded. Scar tissue is causing some of your pain. We need to operate and take care of this situation before complications develop."

"Okay, Dr. Owen, I'm ready."

"Good. We'll schedule the surgery for seven A.M. on Wednesday to give you another day to rest and regain your strength."

The surgeons left and Jay began visualizing the operation as being successful. He could look forward to recovery, even if he did need to stay in the hospital two or three months. He had stayed here over five months the first time, so what difference would it make in his life, if he needed to stay a month or two now in order to regain his health? Excited at the prospect of being able to do his challenging engineering work, he could hardly wait for Wednesday to come. He thanked God for helping him reach the place where he could get the medical treatment he needed to function.

After the operation, Dr. Owen stopped by his room.

"Jay, it was as we suspected, the cause of your trouble was scar tissue. We took care of the problem and you're on your way to a speedy recovery."

A month later, when he went for his x-rays, Dr. Owen's report encouraged him.

"If these x-rays show you to be as healthy as you look, it will mean you're in fine shape."

He returned to the ward, hoping to get the results the following day. That day, then the next passed with no word from the doctor. Unable to sleep and fearing something had gone wrong, he tossed and turned. At dawn, he realized the futility of worry and entrusted everything to God.

After sleeping a short time, he awoke to the familiar voice of Dr. Owen by his side.

"I have good news for you, Jay. You'll be leaving the hospital on Friday. We want you to continue your therapy once a week for another two months; then we'll see you for a complete checkup every two months for a six-month period. We'll continue physical therapy meanwhile, to strengthen your muscles."

"Thanks, Dr. Owen. I'll work hard."

"You can stay at a boardinghouse operated by Miss Annie Price. It's about six or seven blocks from the hospital. Walk a few blocks every day. Then build up your strength until you can walk longer distances."

"Thanks, Dr. Owen. This good news makes me happy."

"I'm sure it does," said Dr. Owen, smiling.

On Thursday he walked to the boardinghouse and introduced himself to Miss Annie Price. Dr. Owen had called ahead to tell her he was coming. Jay found her to be a kind, pleasant-looking lady and instantly felt as if he had known her for years.

As he turned to leave, he said, "I'll move in tomorrow, Miss Annie."

At that moment, a young man his age parked his car out front and came up the walk to the house.

"Mr. Ryan, you and Mr. Hanson should know each other. Your room is across the hall from his," said Miss Annie.

"Russ Hanson, call me Russ," said the young man, extending his hand.

Clasping Russ' hand in a firm handshake, Jay introduced himself. The two talked briefly before Russ went inside and Jay walked back to the hospital.

On Friday afternoon, after Jay had moved in and finished putting his things in place at the boardinghouse, Russ came to his door.

"I need to return these books to the library. Wanta go along?"

"Sure. Thanks for asking, Russ."

At the library, Jay went to the shelves with books on engineering. As he browsed through several titles, trying to decide which would be most helpful for him to review, a young lady came over and said, "Hi, I'm Margaret Page. May I help you?"

Jay glanced up at her and almost lost his cool. The first thing he noticed was that her eyes were the exact same shade of dark blue as his. Perfect, he thought, for her skin tone with hair as black as the darkest night arranged in a Grecian style. Wow! Was this young lady beautiful!

Smiling, he said, "I'm Jay Ryan, and I'd like to check out these books, if I may."

She assisted him and they talked until Russ was ready to go. She was a senior in college, majoring in library science with a minor in interior design. Jay learned she had studied Spanish for three years in school and hoped someday to tour South America. She asked questions faster than he could answer them.

As he was leaving, she said, "I hope you visit the library often and tell us about your life in South America."

"Thanks, I have a lot of catching up to do in my reading about theUnited States. I'll try to stop by every morning."

While walking back to the boardinghouse, Russ teased him, "You made quite a hit with the library staff. Not bad public relations for a guy who's new to the country."

Jay grinned. "Yeah, guess I haven't regressed too much. Thanks, for asking me to go with you."

"I sort of got the idea the two of you hit it off. She appeared as interested in talking with you as you were with her. Who knows what it'll lead to?"

"Yeah, think what I'd have missed if I hadn't gone with you. Besides, she helped me find some good engineering books to review."

Jay kept busy with his exercises by walking the fifteen blocks to the library and to the hospital for his therapy. He was happy he had sold his pickup, otherwise he might have been tempted to drive everywhere. Each day he found himself hurrying to the library with the hope of getting a moment to chat with Margaret and learn more about her.

At the same time, this disturbed him. He found himself thinking less often of Antonita. Had he cared for her as deeply as he thought? Was she engaged and making plans to marry some lucky Peruvian? Though the idea hurt, he wanted her to be happy.

At the end of his second week of daily visits to the library, he asked, "Can you get away long enough to have lunch with me today?"

Margaret smiled and said, "Yes, if you'll wait until 12:30 when I'll be free for an hour."

"Great. Do you know a good place to eat nearby?" Jay asked.

"There's a restaurant down the street about three blocks. They serve family-style meals and the food's good."

At 12:30 she came over, touched Jay's arm, and said, "Let's go, so we'll have time to talk during lunch."

As they hurried, Jay said, "I enjoy the time I spend with you, Margaret. We have a great deal in common. For instance, you like nature, and so do I."

"And we both enjoy tasty food," said Margaret as they entered the restaurant.

The lunch passed much too swiftly to please either Jay or Margaret.

On the way back to the library, Jay said, "Thank you for having lunch with me. I enjoyed every minute. Would you like to meet for lunch every Thursday?"

"Yes, I would," said Margaret.

Jay became busy with various activities and the months passed. After the second two months of tests and examinations, Dr. Owen said, "You've surpassed our hopes for recovery and we are canceling the third and last checkup."

"I haven't words to express my thanks and gratitude for your help, Dr. Owen."

"It's been a pleasure to have a patient like you."

"Thanks, Doctor. I look forward to my new life."

Upon returning to the boardinghouse, Jay found a letter from his South American friend, Enrique:

As engineering students, we learned only the general techniques of explosives and blasting. As you know, most of the Andes mountains are solid rock and there's a need for qualified engineers who can design and estimate blasting work. Sign up for a course in blasting at a university near you, and update your knowledge in order to qualify for a good job.

Jay called the university and found they offered a two-semester course. A few days later he got a letter from them requesting a résumé of his engineering work related to blasting and the use of dynamite in general construction. The letter stated:

> If you have sufficient experience, you can take an examination. If the results show you have the knowledge, your training time may be shortened.

Since he had graduated from a university outside the United States, he needed a copy of his diploma in order to take the examination. He wrote to Enrique and asked him to contact the university for him.

Six weeks later with no word from Enrique, Jay called and learned he was working in a different country and had left no forwarding address. Jay sighed. Without a copy of his diploma, there went his chance to take the exam.

# CHAPTER FIVE

Over lunch one Thursday, Margaret asked, "Had any luck reaching your friend Enrique?"

"No, and I'm concerned. There's not much time left to get a copy of my diploma."

"It would be a shame for you to lose this opportunity to update your training."

"Yes, but what can I do?"

"Do you have a mutual friend living down there who might know where he is?"

Jay's eyes brightened. "Margaret, you're an angel. Thanks for the suggestion. I'll be in luck if I can reach Luis Martinez. If anyone knows where Enrique's living, it'll be Luis. I'll start calling the minute I get to the boardinghouse and see what happens."

After several attempts during the afternoon, he decided Luis must not be home and waited until the dinner hour to call again. This time Luis answered the phone.

Jay asked, "Do you know where Enrique is or have his new address?"

"Yes, I'll get it for you."

As soon as dinner was over at Miss Annie's, Jay thanked her, as usual, for the good meal and hurried to his room. He wrote a letter to Enrique asking him to contact the university for him to get a copy of his diploma.

A week later, he got a note from Enrique that asked him to send the legal permission he needed to represent him and Enrique would take care of this business.

Jay caught the downtown bus the next day and secured the necessary legal paperwork to send to him. Later that month, Enrique wrote back telling him about the trip and his tour:

> I was impressed with your university. After touring it, I went to the person in charge of records and presented the legal paper you sent to represent you. As soon as she found your name on the graduate's list, she gave me the enclosed copy for you. Good luck in your studies.

When the time came to take the university exam, thanks to his prior training and work experiences in South America, Jay passed it with no trouble and was ready to begin his studies.

A challenging course and interesting professors helped him gain the information he needed. Busy with his studies, he had to make time to see and talk with Margaret. He enjoyed their Thursday lunches, which he spent answering her questions about South America and sharing his dreams for accepting a job in one of those countries.

About the time he completed his university courses, Jay heard from Enrique again. It was a note telling him that a major company was advertising for a civil engineer with his experience in blasting.

If Jay had a fault he would admit to, it was that he was a nomad, a wanderer. He was seldom happy staying in one place too long. The "grass" always appeared greener in far away, exotic places and that was where he wanted to go. If there was danger, he welcomed it, even if he knew there was a chance he might get his ears beaten down or lose his life.

Thus he became excited about returning to some South American country, until he realized how much he had to do before leaving the United States. He did not have his passport with the required visas or the necessary shots and vaccination certificates.

When he wrote to Enrique, he included his résumé and asked him to write a letter of recommendation to the company. Soon afterward, he planned to take the downtown bus to the federal building and consulates of Bolivia, Chile, and Peru. These were the South American countries he wanted to enter.

As he was leaving, the phone rang.

"Jay, this is Grandad Bill. I want you to fly over and spend a few days at the ranch. If I send you the money, can you make it?"

Jay hesitated.

"Son, I haven't seen you since you left for England during the war."

"Let me see what I can do, Grandad. I'll call you back tonight."

"Is that a promise?"

"Yes, Grandad."

Later, he recalled all the occasions when he and his family visited his grandad at the ranch. Even as a child he was impressed by the way his grandfather worked his schedule to spend time with them. Thinking of those happy experiences, he decided not to wait until that night to let him know he would make the trip.

When his grandfather answered the phone, Jay said, "I can come for a few days."

"Good. I'll be counting them 'til you get here. Yesterday, I sent you a check for a round-trip ticket. Figured if something happened and you couldn't come, you could still use the money."

His grandfather's generous gift brought tears of gratitude to Jay's eyes. He had no way of knowing how he had managed to save enough for the plane ticket, especially considering the difficulty he was having keeping the ranch. But Grandad always put others first.

Later, as he took the bus downtown, he thought of Margaret. He decided to stop by the library first and tell her that his plans had changed.

"Margaret, I'm leaving to spend a few days with my Grandad at his ranch. I'm sorry I can't be here to take you to lunch on Thursday."

"I'll miss you, but I know you're looking forward to visiting your grandfather."

"While I'm away, how about if I call you some afternoon at the library?"

"We'd never get a chance to talk. Here's my number. Call me at home. My parents want to meet you and suggested I invite you to dinner Saturday night. Since you'll be out of town, we'll put that on hold."

"Would the first Saturday after I return from Grandad's be okay?"

"Perfect," said Margaret.

"Gotta go check on my passport and other things I need to get ready to travel to South America."

The day before Jay was to leave for his grandfather's, the university called.

Their spokesperson said, "We heard you're going to South America to challenge the great Andes. As proof of what you've learned, we'll give you a diploma which will be of more value than a certificate. It will be ready for you next Wednesday morning."

"Thanks," said Jay. "I'm looking forward to receiving it."

To be at the university on Wednesday, he had to change his flight reservation to Thursday. He called his grandfather to tell him about the delay. Then he settled back, hoping the days would pass quickly. Instead, they dragged on and Jay found himself pacing restlessly waiting for Wednesday. The more he thought about it, the more eager he became to pick up the diploma and head for the airport.

Finally the day came. As he held the diploma in his hands, he had to admit it looked quite impressive and would no doubt be helpful in securing a job wherever he worked. He was glad he had followed Enrique's suggestion to get further training in explosives. He would find a need for his skills in the Andes Mountains of South America.

Before leaving the city, Jay wrote to Enrique:

I'll be out of town visiting my grandfather for a few days. It's my only chance to see him, even if I miss out on a job with the South American company. In case they

77

haven't hired someone, I'm interested in coming down for an interview. If you need to call me, I've included Grandad's telephone number.

Even though Jay had difficulty sleeping Wednesday night, while thinking of the changes in his life since he last saw Grandad Bill, he awoke before the alarm rang and got ready to leave for the airport. Soon after he arrived, they were airborne. A three-hour flight to Dallas and a quick change to a commuter plane would take him to Grandad Bill.

As the plane touched down at the small airport, Jay saw someone waving his hat. As he stepped out, there stood Grandad, arms spread wide, ready to give him a hug that would almost leave him breathless.

"Grandad! Am I glad to see you. I thought this day would never come."

"Son, it's a special blessing," said Grandad, his eyes misty. "That day you left for England during the war, I wondered if I'd ever see you again."

"God's been good to us, Grandad."

During the ride to the ranch, Jay said, "I sure appreciate what you've done in giving me this trip. I hope I can do something for you someday."

"My pleasure, Son. Glad I could do it. You're going to find a few improvements on the ranch, despite the fact it's been hard to make a decent living."

"I hope this hasn't put a kink in the economy," Jay said.

"No problem, Son."

After Jay had been at the ranch a week, Enrique called him.

"I talked with the company's general manager. There are others interested in the job. Hopefully, they won't hire anyone until they've interviewed you. Regardless of how it turns out, Jay, you did the right thing choosing to visit your grandfather."

Enrique's optimism encouraged Jay and helped him enjoy the time spent updating Grandad on all that had occurred since their last visit.

While Grandad took his usual nap that afternoon, Jay wrote a long letter to Margaret telling her about the area he was visiting:

It's in an interesting, scenic part of Texas, not far from the Davis Mountains. Grandad is already filling me in on all the Texas history I've missed as a result of growing up out of state. He knows how to tell a good, entertaining story. I'll share a few of his best stories with you when I see you. Just wanted to get this ready for the rural letter carrier when he comes by tomorrow.

The next afternoon, Henry Hempstead, Grandad's cousin, came to visit. As they talked, Jay learned he was president of a large construction company in the United States.

Turning to Jay, he said, "I understand you plan to return to South America. If you're interested in living in the U.S., my company can offer you a good job."

Jay glanced at his grandfather. He saw the look of pure happiness on his face. The job offer sounded interesting, but it would probably be in an office and that was not what he wanted. Even if he did want the job, he was not free to take it.

"I'm sorry, Henry, your offer comes too late. I've already committed myself to a job interview with a South American company. However, I appreciate your offer. It's been a pleasure to meet you and discover I have a cousin I had never met."

"I've looked forward to meeting you, Jay, and I'm proud you're a civil engineer. Your father was one of the engineers in charge of constructing a major dam in this country. While you're here, I'd like to show you the engineering project my company is working on. It'll tell you something about our company, if you ever want a job in the future."

"Sounds like a great idea, Jay!" his grandfather exclaimed.

"How long will it take to drive to the project? Could we do it today?" Jay asked.

"No, it's too late. Bill, do you mind if I stay here tonight?"

"Not at all, that's the thing to do," said Grandad.

Henry and Jay helped do the chores and prepare the evening meal. After eating, they sat around the table talking. Henry was interested in hearing Jay's experiences in other countries.

Finally, Jay's grandfather was about to fall asleep. He said, "Henry, Jay can talk all night and not tell you what he's seen there."

"Is Bill trying to tell us it's time for bed?" Henry asked.

"I think so. How early should we leave in the morning?"

"No later than eight o'clock. It's a hundred miles to the project. As we drive through town, I wanta stop and show you where I live," Henry explained.

"I'll be ready."

After Jay got into bed, he reviewed the events of the day. Although he had come to spend time with Grandad Bill, he was encouraging him to explore job possibilities in the United States. Evidently Grandad was hoping Henry could persuade him to work for his company. Before he resolved the job situation in his mind, he fell asleep and did not wake up until his grandfather called him to breakfast.

Soon after eating a tasty meal of country cured ham with red-eye gravy, fried eggs, and fluffy hot biscuits, along with sweet cream butter and Grandad's wild plum jelly, Henry said, "Jay, if I'm to show you the project, we'd better leave. We'll see you tomorrow afternoon, Bill."

"Good-by, Grandad. I'll help you with the barn repairs when I get back."

"Son, forget everything and enjoy the tour," said his grandfather.

En route to town, Henry said, "Jay, you've no idea how much your visit has cheered up Bill."

"It's one of the nicest things that's happened to me in a long while. Grandad Bill is the greatest encourager I know. His cards and letters to me in the hospital helped me get well faster. I wish I was able to do something to show how much I care for him."

"You're showing your care by spending time with him. Though he'd never admit it, I'm sure he must get lonely."

"Yes, sentimental person that Grandad is, he may have moments of loneliness."

"Jay, have you been noticing the different rock formations along this road? With the exception of these occasional outcroppings, the entire area is one broad expanse of sandstone."

"Yes. I'm enjoying the view," Jay replied.

Henry said, "At the project I plan to show you, we're tunneling through rocky ledges like these. Our purpose is to create an irrigation channel through it. We want to use the tunnel to carry water from a man-made reservoir of several acres. As you can see, once we leave the river country this is a dry area that grows little except prickly pear cacti, mesquite brush, and scrub grasses. With plenty of water available, some of this land might be productive. People in the county wanta find out if it's possible. They're watching and hoping the project will be a success."

"You must have had a number of things happen to attract people's attention and get them interested in a project that will take years to complete," said Jay.

"It's been rough for cattle ranchers to buy feed and some took a loss when they had to sell their places. With irrigation, as we plan it, they can irrigate their hay fields."

"If those small ranchers who are losing their land loved it the way Grandad Bill loves his, it must have been heartbreaking for them."

"Yes, it was a sad time. What made it worse was the fact that ranching was all they knew, and it was hard for them to find other work to support their families."

"Here we are in our quiet little town, Jay, where we all know each other. They're good neighbors, willing to lend a hand when anyone needs help. We'll stop so you can meet Emma. I need to tell her we'll be home for dinner tonight."

Henry turned down a street and said, "Our house is the one with all the oak trees around it. My father said there wasn't a tree anywhere when he bought the property. The first thing he did, even before building the house, was plant those trees. He lived long enough to enjoy their shade."

"If he liked trees, I can imagine how much pleasure they must have given him. They sure add a lot to a house, plus what they contribute to the environment," Jay said.

"They sure do. This place wouldn't be half this pleasant, it it wasn't for these trees. Come on in, Jay."

As he stepped inside the door, Emma came downstairs and Henry introduced Jay to her.

"What a pleasure to have you with us, Jay. After the fantastic stories I've heard Bill tell about you and your experiences, I can't believe I'm seeing the real Jay in person."

Jay smiled, gave her a hug and thanked her for the compliment.

"Emma, we've gotta go if we're gonna get back before dark."

As they left, Jay said, "Henry, on the way to town you mentioned something about another big project your company has been working on with some other companies."

"Yes, that was the first one. It's taken almost two years to complete, but it's been a help to the county. The project we're working on now resulted from the first one. We're coming up to the beginning of the tunnel, Jay. As you can see we're more than halfway to completion. Thus far, it's been the most challenging of any work we've done. I'm going to park over to the side so you can get a glimpse of what we're trying to do."

"Great. I'd like to see it and meet the engineer in charge of the project," said Jay.

"Sure, come on. I'll introduce you," said Henry, leading the way.

"Randy Lewis, wait a second, please. I want you to meet my cousin, Jay Ryan. He's also a civil engineer," said Henry leaving the two men talking.

Randy showed Jay around and shared some of the challenges and successes of the work in progress. Jay complimented him on the excellent job they were doing. Henry rejoined them and said, "Don't wanta hurry you, Jay, but we'd better go grab a sandwich or something to tide us over 'til dinner."

"Good luck on the project, Randy, and thanks for the tour," Jay called.

When they entered the small cafe, Henry warned, "Keep a good appetite for dinner tonight, or Emma will think you don't like her cooking."

As soon as they finished eating, Henry said, "If we leave now, we'll get home before dark. I wanta show you my fish pond and the exquisite water lillies in bloom."

"Great! I'd like to see it," Jay said.

Henry concentrated on his driving, while sharing bits of the state's history from the various historical markers along the road.

Upon reaching the house, he showed Jay to his room, then said, "Let's go see the fish pond. It's where I retreat when I need peace and quiet."

Viewing the beautifully-landscaped garden with its pond of curious gold fish darting among the lilies, Jay said, "It's gorgeous. I can understand how you must enjoy it."

Emma called,"Dinner!" As they sat down, she said, "Jay, I've invited a few friends to come tonight and meet you. They'll join us for dessert."

The dinner could not have been better and Jay was helping clear the table when Henry greeted the first guests and ushered them into the living room.

Interested in learning about the life and customs of people in South America, the guests kept Jay busy answering questions until midnight. As they were leaving, a lady commented, "I love the way you speak. When did you begin learning Spanish?"

"At age two after we arrived in the South American country where my father worked. Spanish was the language I heard everywhere I went. Although we spoke English at home, both my parents could also speak Spanish."

After the last guest left, Jay thanked Henry and Emma for the enjoyable time.

"Glad you got to meet them and exchange views. All of us could have listened to you talk all night, Jay. It's late though. Emma, we better let him get some sleep."

In his room, Jay undressed and got into bed. It was the first day he was too busy to think of Margaret or Antonita. Though what Antonita did was no business of his, in the stillness of the night she crept into his thoughts. Perhaps it was due to his strong desire to return to work in South America.

# Chapter Six

As he lay awake reflecting on his life in South America, Jay became more eager to return there to work. He recalled happenings while on a scientific expedition and the night they caught an unauthorized person using their short wave radio.

After this spy incident, the chief had said, "There are those who would like to see us fail. Let us strive to make this a successful and worthwhile venture."

Their exploratory days in the jungle held potential for all kinds of life-threatening dangers from disease, wild animals, unfriendly tribal people, or floods caused by torrential rains and rivers overflowing their shallow banks. Though he contracted yellow fever, God helped him recover.

The living room clock struck three times. Jay couldn't believe he had lain awake such a long while. He pushed aside past events and went to sleep.

At breakfast, Emma asked if he had rested well.

Jay said, "Yes, once I put South America on hold. Sharing my experiences in those countries last night led me to recall events I hadn't thought of in years."

As soon as breakfast was over, Henry said, "We'll take one of the scenic routes to the ranch. Our mountains aren't as high or picturesque as the Andes, but they have a certain beauty. There's an observatory on the highest mountain. Astronomers from our country and several others make observations there of celestial phenomena. It's a busy place year-round, especially in the summer. Bus and car loads of people from the states, as well as foreign countries and territories, drive up to the top where the observatory sits. On a clear day, you can see over 200 miles in any direction from where you stand on this mountain."

"It sounds like a fantastic view," said Jay. "Wish I could stay longer and go visit the area, but I can't. This trip to Grandad's and your home has shown me how little I know about the land of my birth. While I live in my home country, I want to learn more about it. Before we leave, Henry, thank you and Emma again for your kindness, and all you have done to make this a pleasant and memorable experience for me."

The scenic route proved to be as spectacular as Henry claimed. They left the flat plain and climbed higher and higher, as the road led up and around the mountains.

"You're in antelope and deer country, Jay," said Henry. "You might spot them grazing on some higher slope."

Keeping a sharp lookout for antelope, Jay had almost given up seeing one when he discovered ten grazing on the side of the opposite mountain. On the way down he saw two deer sipping water from a small stream flowing parallel to the road.

He glanced at Henry and said, "This was a great idea to drive the scenic route. I enjoy nature and the outdoors. Seeing those beautiful animals was special for me."

Soon they left the mountains and once again drove through mostly flat and treeless country. A few miles farther, they reached the dirt road leading to Grandad Bill's ranch. He was in the kitchen getting ready to eat when they entered.

"Help yourselves, boys. There's plenty."

After eating, Henry said, "Bill, sorry I can't stay longer. Gotta get back to the office. Thanks for encouraging Jay to come with me to see our work and visit us. When you're this way again, Jay, stop by our place."

"Thanks, Henry, I will. Thanks for everything and good luck on the project."

Jay and his grandfather lingered at the table talking. "I can never thank you enough for sending me money for my ticket, Grandad."

"Son, it's been wonderful having you here. I'm glad I could do it."

"This trip has been great. It's given me a chance to meet Henry and see the kind of work his company does. It's helped me learn more about my country as I've seen how people work together to upgrade their quality of life. Which reminds me, I promised to help you repair the barn while I'm here."

"I got the barn repaired yesterday, Son. Joe Bayley, my neighbor, came over and we finished it in half a day. He stayed to dinner, then went home. As long as I keep my cooking skills, I seem to have no trouble getting volunteer help."

"You're something else, Grandad! Nobody bakes good sourdough yeast bread like you. I remember Dad saying if it wasn't so far, he would come all the way from South America for a slice of your bread with sweet cream butter."

His grandfather chuckled and said, "Yeah, I baked three loaves today. Son, I've been thinking about what we can do tomorrow. You'll be leaving in a couple of days. Wanta try fishing in the morning?"

"That would be super, Grandad. It will be like the old days. How about bait? You used to raise earthworms for fishing."

"Still raise 'em in an old tub. All we need do in the morning is put the earthworms in a can of moist dirt, load our old bamboo fishing poles on the pickup, and we're ready to go."

The happy pair spent the afternoon recalling incidents and events of the past. Soon it was time to do chores and the evening meal. After eating and doing the dishes, they went out and sat down on the long veranda.

The western sun, a brilliant orange ball, sank lower and lower in the sky until they no longer saw it. Then came Jay's favorite time of day: twilight, the interval between sunset and darkness. He and his grandfather had much in common; they enjoyed the outdoors and nature. Each relaxed with his own thoughts as the peace and quiet of the day crept in. Grandad Bill broke the silence.

"Jay, you have no idea what happiness you've brought me by your visit. Each time you come, I try to store everything you say and do in my memory bank. It helps to ease the loneliness after you leave."

"Grandad, there have been times in my life when I wondered if I would live to see you again. This visit with you has been a special blessing for me and I thank God."

"Yes, Son, life is short. We both have much for which we should thank God."

As night came on, Jay's grandfather yawned, "If we're gonna get an early start on the fishing trip tomorrow, we better get to bed."

"Good idea, Grandad. I've had trouble staying awake the past hour. I'm used to getting to bed by nine o'clock. Last night it was after one before I got there, so I'll say good night."

Back in his room, Jay realized he had only written one letter to Margaret, and he had forgotten to call her as he had promised. Regardless of what came up, he must call her the following night.

The next morning when he awoke, his grandfather had breakfast cooked, lunch packed, and the pickup loaded with fishing gear.

"We'll be ready to leave, Son, the minute we get through eating."

Eager to leave for the dam where they planned to fish, they did not linger over the meal. Once underway, the smooth road of the flat country changed to deep ruts and chuck holes as they reached the hills.

"If we're lucky, we can make it," said Jay's grandfather, stopping short of a caved-in culvert.

"Grandad, we can't drive any farther. We'd better head back home."

"No way!" his grandfather exclaimed. "We can't give up and miss having fish for supper tonight. We'll leave the pickup here and walk to the dam. It's about a mile."

When they got there a short while later, Jay's grandfather smiled and said,"Gonna be a perfect day for fishing."

His prediction came true. The instant they put their lines in the water, the fish began biting. Soon they caught their limit and headed for where they left the pickup.

When they got home, they hurried through the chores then came in to cook supper.

Jay said, "I'll build the fire, then help you clean the fish."

"Son, soon as the fire's burning good, I'll have these perch ready for the pan."

"That's what I like to hear. I'm getting hungrier by the minute thinking how much I'm gonna enjoy this special treat you've planned for me, Grandad."

"My pleasure, Son."

After eating and doing dishes, they went out on the veranda to watch the sunset. Grandad sat in a comfortable old rocker and Jay sat in another close by.

Twilight came.

Then darkness.

It was a moment of mixed emotions for both Jay and his grandfather; happiness at being together, and sadness at the thought of being separated.

Grandad said, "It's a two-hour drive to the airport, and your plane leaves at 9:15."

"Grandad, before I go to bed, would you mind if I use your phone to call a young lady?"

"Is it serious, Son?"

"No, but she's a marvelous young lady. I'd like you to meet her. You two would get along great."

"Go ahead, Son. I'm heading for bed. Good night."

"Good night, Grandad, and thanks."

Dialing Margaret's phone number, Jay was disappointed when he heard a busy signal. After four attempts, he finally got through and said, "Margaret, this is Jay. I just wanted to tell you I've missed you and hope to see you tomorrow afternoon."

"What time are you due in Grand Junction?" Margaret asked.

"Two P.M., I think. I don't have my ticket handy to check. Take care and I'll stop by the library on my way to the boardinghouse."

He lost no time getting to bed and going to sleep.

At five A.M. his grandfather woke him to eat. Before going to breakfast, Jay put the same amount of money Grandad sent him for his plane ticket, under the pillow for him to find after he was gone. When they finished eating, he loaded his luggage and they left for the airport.

As they drove, Jay smiled and said, "Thanks again, Grandad, for all you've done to make these few days with you so marvelous."

His grandfather's voice quivered. "I'll treasure the memory of your visit, Son."

Putting his arm around his grandfather's shoulder, Jay said, "During those months I was in the hospital, I recalled the great times we had when we came to visit you from South America. Thinking about them helped me try harder to recover from my wounds. If all goes well with my job interview and I make some money, I'll send you a round-trip ticket to come visit me for as long as you want in those beautiful countries."

"Thank you, Jay. I admire you for the good heart you've always had. God bless you and don't forget your old Grandad."

They arrived in time for Jay to check his luggage, say farewell, and board the plane.

As the plane became airborne, a wave of sadness swept over him. Only God knew if he would see his grandfather again.

During the flight, Jay reflected on the days spent with Grandad Bill. How he had enjoyed his stories and the way he could blend facts and humor to tell a good yarn. Until his visit he had not realized how little he knew about United States and Texas history, but grandad's knowledge had so intrigued and impressed him, he was determined to learn more about it. He decided that after he reached home, he would go to the city library and read books and periodicals about the country. An added benefit would be getting to see and talk with Margaret. He leaned back in the seat and smiled. Eager to study about his grandfather's heroes in American history and see Margaret again, he could not wait for the plane to land.

As soon as he stepped off the plane, he got his luggage and left for the boardinghouse. Later, he walked to the library.

When he entered, Mrs. Hargrove, head librarian, said, "We've missed you. Thanks for the cards you sent."

Margaret said, "They've given me a bad time about you since you've been away."

"Yes," said Mrs. Hargrove, "We told her you'd meet a Texas beauty and probably stop visiting the library."

In mock seriousness, Jay asked, "How could you people say such things? Actually, now that I think about it, I never went where there were any young ladies."

Margaret said, "Jay, your letter about life on the ranch sounded as if you enjoyed the visit with your grandfather."

"I did. He's a history buff and remembers every histori-cal event that's taken place during his lifetime. As a result of growing up in South America, I know so little about my own country. While I'm here I want to study and learn all I can about it."

"This is a good place to begin," said Margaret. She led him to the rows of books on the United States from politics to wars and said, "You'll probably want to begin with the American Revolution and our fight for independence. Then the "War between the States," that's what it's called up north. States in the south refer to it as the Civil War."

"Hm, I hadn't realized the difference," said Jay. "Both my parents came from Texas. If you have some books on Texas' Battle for Independence, the American Revolution, or anything else that'll help me learn about my country, great."

"We do, Jay. I'll get them for you," said Margaret.

When Margaret returned with the books Jay had re-quested, he remarked,"So they gave you a bad time, huh?"

"Yes, but just until I got your letter, then they stopped teasing."

"Did you miss me while I was out of town, Margaret?"

"Yes I did and I'm glad you're back. Remember, you're coming to dinner Saturday night at seven, but I'll drive by for you at five. My family can't wait to meet you."

"I'm looking forward to meeting them," he said and left for the boardinghouse.

He began reading. When Miss Annie called him to eat, he was still reading. The minute he finished the meal, he said good night and returned to his room to read some more. He wanted to see if General Sam Houston and his soldiers succeeded in surprising General Santa Ana and his troops, while taking their afternoon siesta. Grandad had told him that anecdote. As the grandfather clock struck two, he reluctantly closed the book and went to bed.

It seemed he barely got to sleep when Miss Annie called,"Breakfast!"

While they ate, Russ Hanson joined them. After filling his plate, he asked, "How was the visit with your grandfather?"

"Couldn't have been better. Only problem was the time slipped by too fast. Miss Annie, I'm touring the city today and won't be here for lunch," said Jay.

"Neither will I, Miss Annie. I'm meeting with a couple interested in buying a farm near the county line."

When the meal was over, Jay walked up the street to the bus stop. It came shortly and he boarded. At the next bus stop, a well-dressed gentleman entered and took a seat beside Jay.

"You must live in the city," Jay remarked.

"No, I'm visiting my son and his wife. While they're at work, I'm touring the city."

"So am I. I grew up in South America. On this tour, I've found that the similarities between the modern buildings of South American cities and the United States ended when the bus left the business section. For instance, in most South American cities, blocks of houses are joined together and their roofs are finished only at different elevations. Here in the U. S., most houses are at least twenty feet apart and often have a fence to define the property line."

"You must've had some interesting experiences living in those countries."

"Yes, one occurred shortly after the war, when I returned to South America to work. The first time I rode a bus to my job, I lost my wallet because I had it in my back pocket. It should have been inside my jacket pocket with the zipper closed."

"What a shock it must have been."

"A lesson I never forgot. It would've been worse if I hadn't been told to carry copies of all important identification cards instead of the originals. That was the best advice I ever got."

"Would it have taken long to replace them?"

"It sure would, plus the cost. To give you an idea of how it was then, I'll tell you a story. In one country pickpockets were causing all kinds of problems. The national police chief asked the American consulate for suggestions to slow down the thievery. They arranged for an FBI agent to meet with him. The FBI agent asked if he could talk with a jailed pickpocket.

"In the office section of the jail they visited, there was a long counter. While the FBI agent and the national police chief stood on one side, the pickpocket was brought in to stand opposite them. The agent was facinated by the intricate motions the man's fingers made and how he moved his eyes without turning his head.

"After answering a variety of questions, he asked the agent, 'Do you have the time?' When the agent reached inside his pocket, a puzzled look swept over his face. He asked the pickpocket, 'What happened? My watch is missing!'

'Señor, I was showing you what I was trying to tell you. Here's your watch,' said the pickpocket."

"That was something else. Think you'll go back to South America?"

"Yes, if I can get a job there. It's an adventure living and working in those countries. They offer great opportunities for success to the good, decent professionals who come there to live. People are friendly and if you treat them right, they'll respond favorably."

"I've enjoyed talking with you and wish we could talk longer, but I must get off at the next stop."

"It's been a pleasure for me, too," said Jay.

When Jay reached his stop later, he got off. He was delighted that he'd found someone with whom he could share his experiences. On the way to the boardinghouse, he wondered why there had been no word from Enrique. Had the company hired an engineer and he was hesitant to tell him?

Two weeks passed. He could no longer stand the suspense and decided to call. But before he could, Miss Annie knocked on his door.

Smiling, she said, "Perhaps this letter will brighten your day."

"Thanks, Miss Annie, I hope so."

A quick glance at the letter told him why Enrique had postponed writing:

> The country has issued a decree stating that no business or company can have over ten-percent foreigners on their payroll. The company that has offered you a job already has over sixteen-percent. At the moment, everything is in turmoil because the foreigners they have are highly skilled professionals. When I met with their general manager, I learned they have decided to make the changes to meet the requirements. It may take several months for them to get this problem solved.

Jay could not afford to sit around waiting months or years for the company to hire him. He needed a job to support himself. The next three weeks, he studied the ads but didn't find anything of interest.

One evening Miss Annie stopped by his open door to give him the *Evening News*. He took the paper and went to the front porch. While he sat studying the ad section, Russ came up the walk whistling a cheery tune.

"You must've had a good day."

"Made a sale been working on a long time."

Jay continued reading the ads until he finished the last page and had found nothing of interest. Then he saw it. Could this be the answer to his prayers?

Wanted, project engineer for constructing road to new ski lodge in the mountains. One with knowledge and experience preferred.

A post office box number was listed. It looked promising. Tucking the paper under his arm, he went inside as Miss Annie called, "Dinner's ready."

Jay helped her with her chair and sat down.

Russ began the conversation with, "I've found one can't be too careful these days."

"Too careful about what?" Jay asked.

"Clothes. Believing I was well-dressed yesterday, I was surprised when a couple asked, 'Are you aware your shoes don't match?'"

"I've never heard the like. What did you tell them?" Miss Annie asked.

"Thinking they were kidding, I glanced down and saw that even though my shoes were similar, one was black and the other tan."

"That showed you were prosperous, Russ," Jay told him. "I've lived and worked in areas where people could afford only one pair of shoes. They carried them in their arms and walked barefoot to town. Before reaching the plaza, they put on their shoes."

"Mercy!" exclaimed Miss Annie. "We should be grateful for what we have and never complain about anything."

After they finished eating, Jay said, "Miss Annie, I won't be here tomorrow night. I'm having dinner with Margaret Page and her family at their home."

"Fine young lady and from a good family," said Miss Annie.

"I think so," said Jay.

He hurried to his room and wrote a letter to answer the ad. He enclosed a copy of his résumé so he could drop it in the mail tomorrow. It was now a matter of trusting God and waiting to hear from the company.

# CHAPTER SEVEN

O n Saturday afternoon, Jay spent more time deciding what he should wear to dinner at Margaret's house. After changing his clothes twice, he chose his dark suit, white shirt with french cuffs, and his favorite red silk tie. He finished dressing as Margaret arrived.

As he hurried to meet her, Miss Annie said, "You look handsome, Jay."

"Thanks. I hope Margaret and her family will be pleased with me."

"You be your best self and don't worry," Miss Annie told him.

As he got into the car, he asked, "Am I dressed all right for the occasion?"

"Perfect. You look elegant. Sorry I'm late. Had trouble getting away."

"What happened? Did your parents not want me to come to dinner?"

"No, nothing like that. I told you they can't wait to meet you. The problem was my brothers wanted to come with me."

"Well, why didn't you bring them?"

"Because I wanted these moments alone with you."

"What you said makes me believe you like having me around," Jay said.

"I do, and I hate to think of you accepting a job out of town."

"Margaret, I have to support myself. If an out-of-town job is all that's available and it's the kind of work I can do, I'll take it."

"I understand. Before we reach the house, I want to tell you how excited my parents are about meeting you. This is the first time my boyfriend is not someone they already know."

"Interesting. Think they'll like me?"

"Of course they'll like you. You're a likable person, Jay. Trouble is my brothers are at the stage where they can make a nuisance of themselves. They'll probably want you to tell them a story about your childhood."

"I have plenty I can tell. They might like the one about my pet burros and how they escaped being eaten by a hungry cougar."

"They'd love it. However, you'd better explain what a cougar is before they ask."

"Sure, no problem. What disturbs me is that we never have enough time together."

"I know. I could listen to you talk forever, you've had such interesting experiences. Even if you live to be a hundred, you'll never get around to sharing them all."

"Thanks, Margaret. Are you aware, you're the first and only girl I've dated since I left the hospital?"

"No, I didn't know. I'm glad you told me. I haven't dated anyone else since my first date with you."

"Great. I'm happy you haven't. Who knows what plans God has for our lives? We'll have to be patient and wait."

Margaret turned into a residental district of well-kept houses and neat yards. As she parked in the driveway, two young boys crowded each other through the front door and raced toward the car.

Before Margaret could introduce them, the oldest said, "Hello, my name's Denis and this is my brother Frank."

"Good to meet you," Jay said, getting out of the car and shaking hands with the boys.

"How old are you, Denis?"

"Eleven."

Before Jay could ask, Frank said, "I'm nine."

The boys ran ahead to the front door and opened it wide, permitting Margaret and Jay to enter.

Margaret said, "Dad and Mother, I want you to meet Jay Ryan." Turning to Jay, she said, "This is my dad, Stanley, and my mother, Ruth. You've already met my brothers, Denis and Frank."

"Welcome to our home, Jay. Margaret has shared such interesting stories of your life, we feel we already know you," he said

Margaret and Jay sat down on the love seat, while her brothers selected chairs close by.

Mrs. Page said, "If you will excuse me, I'll get dinner on the table."

"Need my help, Mother?"

"Not yet. I'll call if I do."

"Mr. Ryan, my sister said you tell stories about where you grew up. Would you tell us one, please?" Denis asked.

Jay glanced at Margaret. "Is there time to tell the boys a short one?"

"Yes. Go ahead," she told him.

"When I was your age, I lived on a ranch in Peru. It was so far from the nearest town, it took us two days to get there."

"In a car?" Denis asked.

"Riding horseback along a narrow trail that wound up through the mountains and crossed rivers."

"Wow!" both boys exclaimed.

"One day, my dad bought two small burros named Zack and Zoro. When they came to the ranch, the horses didn't want them around. It didn't bother the little burros. They kept to themselves and roamed wherever they wanted to graze. Regardless of how far they strayed, when night came on they headed to the corral.

"Once they didn't make it back. The thought of a hungry cougar eating them made shivers run down my spine. At bedtime I looked out my window and called, 'Zack and Zoro, I miss you. Please keep safe and come home.' Unable to sleep, I tossed and turned thinking of my little pets out in the wild with no protection from wild animals.

"Then I heard a loud 'Onk—ee—onk—onk!' I ran over to the window and listened. It grew quiet. Three times during the night, they woke me with their 'Onk—ee—onk—onk!' braying sound. I decided they were trying to let me know where they were. I tried not to worry about them.

"At dawn, I dressed, took my 22 rifle, and walked through the brush that tore my clothing and scratched my face, until I came to a site between three mountains. As I crept forward, I spotted Zack and Zoro standing close together, their gaze fixed on something in the shadows. Just then they uttered such a fearful cry, I glanced to where they looked. I saw a young cougar ready to attack. I fired my twenty-two. Ping! The bullet hit a rock. The cougar jumped as if he had been hit. In three leaps, he disappeared behind some high boulders. After their scary experience, Zack and Zoro never again stayed out late."

"Thanks for a neat story," said the boys.

Mrs. Page, called, "Everyone please come to the dining room. Dinner is served."

Mr. Page kept the conversation going by asking Jay questions of what it was like to live and work in South America.

After dinner, Margaret and her mother cleared the table and everyone returned to the living room. The evening passed much too quickly. Suddenly it was the boys' bedtime.

Not wanting to overstay his first visit, Jay said, "Margaret, before it gets much later, could I trouble you to take me to the boardinghouse?"

"Yes, we should leave now. Mother and Dad will worry about me if I'm driving home late at night."

Turning to Margaret's parents, Jay said, "Thanks for inviting me to dinner tonight. I've enjoyed every minute and the meal was super, but I need to get back."

As they drove along, Jay said, "Margaret, your family is precious. I'm happy I got to meet and talk with them."

"So am I. A week from today, the family has planned a picnic and fishing trip to the river. Keep your calendar clear as you'll be my special guest," said Margaret.

At the boardinghouse, Jay put his arms around Margaret and gave her a lingering kiss before saying, "Much as I'd like to have you stay longer, I can't. Be careful and hurry back to the house, okay?"

"I will, Jay."

"Tell your parents thanks again for the lovely evening in their home. It was great. I'll see you Monday at the library," he said, getting out and waving before going inside.

On the way to his room, he passed by Miss Annie reading in her rocker. She asked, "How was your evening, Jay?"

"Perfect! One of the nicest evenings I've spent in a long while."

"I knew it would be," she said.

The following Thursday morning, an answer came from Jay's inquiry. Trevor Price of Diamon Construction Company in Canon City, Colorado, called.

"Mr. Ryan, you sound as if you're the engineer for the job we've contracted. If you're still interested, we'll get a round-trip ticket in the mail to you today."

"I'm interested, and I'll leave as soon as I get the plane ticket."

"Good! Your reservations will be made for Tuesday at 9:15 A.M. We'll take care of all your expenses while you're here. I'll meet you at the airport and take you to the hotel."

The instant Jay replaced the receiver, he bowed his head and gave thanks to God. Then he headed for the library to tell Margaret his good news.

Margaret said, "I know you're happy and you need the job, but I hate to see you go."

"Don't be sad, Margaret. I'm not leaving the United States. I'll still be here Saturday to go on the family picnic with you."

"Don't worry about getting to the airport on Tuesday. I'll take you."

"Margaret, I hate to trouble you," Jay protested. "I can take the bus."

"I'm sure you can, but I want to take you."

"In that case, great. I'll relax and browse through the new magazines until it's time to take you to lunch. You didn't forget did you?"

"No. I'll be ready."

Before he returned to the boardinghouse, Jay checked out what he needed for his interview. That night at dinner he bubbled over as he explained how he would fly out early Tuesday morning for a job interview.

Russ said, "I'll take you to the airport."

"Thanks, Russ. I've already accepted Margaret's offer."

On Saturday morning, Jay had no sooner eaten breakfast and dressed, when Margaret arrived at eight o'clock.

He came out with a large bag of marshmallows. "If we get a fire started, I thought the boys might have fun toasting these."

"They will, Jay, and they'll be happy you thought of them."

At the Page home, Jay helped carry the picnic supplies to their station wagon.

He said, "I'm reminded of the day we loaded our supplies for an Amazon River trip."

"Did you really take a trip down the Amazon?"

"Yes, I did."

"Then you'll have to tell us about it."

Sitting by Jay in the back seat, Margaret said, "This trip won't be as exciting as yours, but I hope you'll enjoy it."

"I'm sure I will," Jay assured her.

As they drove along, Mr. Page said, "We're going to a picnic site on a small river. A bridge washed out with part of the road, so the highway department keeps the crossing shallow and the river bottom free of holes. Until the new bridge is finished, traffic uses this shallow crossing to reach the other side. It's such a busy place every weekend, a park ranger directs the traffic."

Upon reaching the river, Mr. Page asked the ranger, "May we park to the side to eat our lunch?"

"Yes, just be sure you're off the road," the ranger told him.

As they were eating, a speeding car ignored the ten-miles-per-hour speed limit and broke through the barricade. It landed half-submerged among some large boulders. Jay saw that the swift current was threatening to tip the car over, so he jumped into the river on one side of the car. The park ranger joined him on the other side and they worked to stabilize it. The frightened passengers tugged at the doors to try to force them open.

"Keep the doors closed or the current will drag you down river! We can get you out if you'll stay inside!" Jay shouted, before diving under water and coming up with a large rock. Grasping it firmly, he smashed the rear window and cleared away the broken pieces, while the ranger kept the car steady.

"Come out one at a time," he ordered as the passengers crowded toward the opening. As they freed them, Mr. Page led them through the cold water to safety. The driver staggered toward the opening. Jay caught him by the arm and dragged him out. Seconds later the car slid from the rocks and into a deep hole.

"Thanks for your help. I'm calling the State Patrol to investigate the accident," said the ranger.

Mr. Page and Margaret brought mugs of hot coffee for them. While Mr. Page sipped his, Mrs. Page came over with a large bedspread.

"Stan, get those wet clothes off and wrap this around you, or you'll get pneumonia."

"Very well," he said, going to change.

When the boys saw how funny he looked, they doubled over laughing.

"Jay, drive us across to the picnic site. It takes both my hands to keep this garb on."

Jay and the boys found one with a fireplace. They gathered dry twigs and he taught them how to build a camp fire. Mrs. Page draped her husband's trousers over an old camp stool to dry.

The boys toasted marshmallows and Jay began talking about his trip down the Great Amazon.

"It was a trip planned with two college friends who were also studying to be civil engineers. After we got our parents' permission to take a year off of college, we began planning how to get our act together. We had to work out the details and plans for building a strong raft that would be our living quarters for six months or longer. It would have to be river and sea worthy and be able to survive any storms. We built it from native materials we found near the Amazon headwaters.

"Our adventure called for money we didn't have. John's father observed how we weren't earning much from odd jobs, so he loaned us what we needed. Meanwhile, a South American magazine, published in both Spanish and English, heard about our plans and bought all rights to the story of our venture. It was enough to repay John's father what he'd loaned us.

"Our next hurdle was getting to South America. We worked our way on a Grace Line Ship, *The Santa Maria*. We helped with what needed to be done."

"Jay, was the captain curious about what you were doing?" asked Margaret.

"He asked, 'Couldn't you find something exciting without looking for death in the jungle?' I said the adventure we've planned should be first class, despite the possibility of getting tropical diseases, meeting unfriendly tribes, or whatever comes our way.

"Travel by freighter is slow. When we reached our destination several months later, Port Mollendo, Peru, it was a challenge to keep the port names and their countries in order. After we landed, we loaded our gear onto a freight truck. It took us seven days riding over dirt roads to arrive in Cuzco, Peru, where my parents lived. We rested a couple of days, then left by train on the first part of our trip. The second part of our travel was by freight truck. The third part was the toughest. We walked five days over muddy jungle trails and behind the pack mules that carried our gear. We traveled by canoe with some Indians for four days down the Ucayali River to the Great Pongo. We were nearing the headwaters of the Amazon."

Mr. Page said, "Everybody into the station wagon, it's getting late. We'll go home and have somethng to eat, then Jay can finish telling us the story."

# CHAPTER EIGHT

After they got back onto the main road, Mr. Page asked, "Where are the fishing poles?"

"On top of the car. We never took them down," said Frank.

Denis said, "There were too many exciting things happening to stop and fish. Was it like this floating down the Amazon on your raft?"

Jay smiled and said, "No, but it had its exciting moments."

The boys fell asleep and all was quiet until twin deer appeared in the middle of the road. Mr. Page dimmed the lights and pulled over to the side.

"Poor little creatures. They're too young to fend for themselves. Something must have happened to their mother, or else they would not be alone."

An instant later, the fawns disappeared into the thick underbrush.

All was quiet until Margaret asked, "Did this remind you of life on your ranch?"

"Yes, of a fawn I found after a cougar killed his mother. I took him home, fed and cared for him until he grew up, and then I returned him to the wild. An adorable little pet, I let him sleep at the foot of my bed those first few days. He wandered into the kitchen as the cook peeled white potatoes for lunch. He grabbed a peeling and began eating. Every morning he waited for his treat."

When they got home, the boys awoke, hopped out of the car, and took the fishing poles to the garage. Denis put the worms for fish bait into his mother's flower bed. Margaret and her mother hurried to get the meal ready, while Mr. Page and Jay unloaded the car.

As soon as they came inside, Mrs. Page called, "Food's on the table."

No one lingered over the meal. They were eager to hear the rest of Jay's story.

When they were all seated in the living room, Mr. Page asked,"Where did we leave off, Jay?"

"We were nearing the headwaters of the Amazon. After hiking five days, we had reached the end of the horse trail. A large farmhouse stood across the river from us. The next morning we watched as two men left the farm house and rowed over to us. As they came ashore, we learned one man's father owned the large farm. They had come to take our cargo across. We were to wait there for a group of Indians to arrive and guide us down river to the Great Pongo."

"Jay, how did these people know to meet you?" asked Mrs. Page.

"Earlier, we'd contacted governors of the states we'd be traveling through, and asked them to write letters of recommendation to people who might help us.

"We had a marvelous visit as guests of the Señor Rios family. We saw unusual jungle creatures on their land. At first glimpse, what we thought was a human child in the water turned out to be a giant frog. It came ashore and hopped up on a rock.

"We had brought gifts of mirrors, knives, pocketknives, metal files, and fishing hooks for the Indians, so I asked Señor Rios if they liked them and he said they did. Later, when the Indians guided us down river, we admired how skilled the male and female crew members of our flotilla were. When we reached the Pongo, however, they would guide us no farther.

"We traded a machete for a canoe and got two Indians to help me navigate it, since I wanted the excitement of going through the gorge. We tied rope loops around the canoe to have something to grasp if it flipped over. Wearing life jackets, we started down river. We were nearly through the gorge when we got too close to a whirlpool and the worst happened."

"Oh, no!" Margaret cried. "What did you do?"

"We held on to the rope loops, got the canoe up, climbed in, and paddled hard until we shot out in fast swirling water to a lake."

"Whoee. It must have seemed much longer than it took," said Mr. Page.

"Twelve minutes in our speeding canoe, which felt like it might go airborne. We set up camp to gather available materials and build our raft with the simple tools we had. Can you imagine what it was like cutting down balsa and palm trees and splitting them into boards for a raft with living quarters, kitchen, clay stove, and a piranha-proof swiming pool?"

"I can see it was no ordinary raft," said Margaret.

Mr. Page said, "I'm wondering how you navigated something that size."

"We used two long poles and paddles to push and navigate its course in the main channel. Our anchor was a twenty-pound rock tied to a rope."

"You haven't told us how long it took to build," Margaret reminded him.

"Forty-three days to get it ready to launch and start floating down river."

"One of our greatest challenges was staying in the Ucayali River's main channel. On the third day after we launched the raft, we entered the wrong channel. We drifted for hours, dodging sandbars, until we eventually landed on one.

'So much for our great adventure,' Paul sighed.

'I never dreamed this could happen,' said John. 'Now what'll we do?'

'It's a matter of being patient and waiting. Volumes of water reach this river only days after a rain storm, causing it to flood. When that happens, it'll get here and lift us off this sandbar.'

'You sound so positive, Jay. I wish I could believe you,' said John.

'If this was the United States, somebody would alert the Coast Guard and they'd come looking for us,' said Paul.

John said, 'We're not in the United States. We don't know where we are.'"

'We have maps showing our location. God knows knows where we are. He has not forgotten us and is probably working out something to help us. I've lived much of my life in isolated places and observed how nature solves problems.'

"On the third night we were stranded, we felt a jerk. The raft finally broke free and we began floating downstream to the main channel shown on our map. Happy we were moving again, John and Paul kept telling each other, 'We're floating!' Five days later, we came to some native huts near the river bank. We steered the raft to shore and anchored.

"Leaving Paul with the raft, John and I took a few gifts and paddled ashore in our dinghy. We found a crowd waiting. I bowed low, shook hands with everyone, then opened a bag and gave out gifts."

"How did you communicate with them?" Mrs. Page asked.

"Through sign language. Guess we didn't do too bad. When we left we had a load of bananas, papayas, yuca, and a pet monkey that rode in my shirt pocket."

"Did you buy the little monkey?" asked Denis.

"No, a boy gave him to us. Courtesy demanded we graciously accept his gift. Our days were much the same along the Upper Ucayali, except for stops to visit the Indians. The river took different names as it increased in size. It was called the Upper Ucayali when it joined Rio Marañon. From there to its junction with Rio Negro, its name is the Upper Amazon; and from Rio Negro on it's called the Great Amazon River or Lower Amazon.

"Some steamboats offered to tow us as we floated down the river, but our raft was not ready for towing. When we got to Iquitos, we bought what we needed to do the job. It took us nearly a week to do the work and add the required navigational lights.

"Soon after we left Iquitos, a small tug towing a scow and a float, pulled over to help us reach Rio Negro in twenty-six days. The tug was going to Manaus, a large city upstream. Since we'd decided we were going all the way to the Atlantic Ocean, we thanked him and stayed in the main stream."

"Jay, did you find the Great Amazon as you'd imagined it?" Margaret asked.

"No, it exceeded my wildest imagination. I was amazed to find it was so wide in places, we were unable to see the shore.

"Then we came to something we had looked forward to seeing and feeling. A tidal wave five feet high and reaching six hundred miles up the Amazon, almost capsized the raft. We had reached Obidos, a tidal landmark. Water splashed over us. Our things would have been swept overboard, if we had not secured them earlier.

"The next morning we watched as a small boat intercepted our path, something no other boat had done. The man pulled alongside, jumped over, and tied to the raft. He introduced himself in Portuguese, the language of Brazil. He belonged to a group of volunteers who took turns patrolling the river for anyone in trouble.

"He was interested in learning about our trip and invited us to breakfast on his boat. While we ate, he said, 'I see your raft has been prepared for towing. We'll tow you to the Atlantic.'

"We couldn't believe it. I told him, 'Señor José, before your offer, we stayed such a long while in the same area. We were beginning to wonder if the Great Amazon would take us to the Atlantic.'

"He insisted we take our meals with him and his crew while he towed us to Belém, the capital of the state. His father, Señor Ramiro Pinedo, was the governor. By the time we reached Belém, it had been 121 days since we left my parents' home in Cuzco of the high Andes. At the dock we were given a policeman to guard our possessions.

"The next morning, José came early to tell us, 'Get cleaned up and dressed for a party. It's been organized in your honor, at the suggestion of my father.'

"Knowing how well South Americans do things, I knew we must be dressed for a state banquet. Since we had nothing but casual clothes with us, we left to get our hair cut and shop for the proper dress clothes and accessories.

"At nine, José came to take us to the party. Seeing how handsome he looked, we were glad we'd bought new clothes, even if it had taken most of our money. The state banquet was an elegant occasion with the governor and other dignitaries in attendance.

"We had one slip-up. We neglected to stop at Leticia, the port of entry. Since José was towing us, we thought nothing of it, until some officers reported it at the party.

José said, 'I towed them almost 600 miles. They're students from the United States wanting the experience of floating the Amazon.' Governor Pinedo quickly came over to our table and took care of the situation.

"During the course of the evening, John, Paul, and I were each asked to speak. The question- and-answer period following our talks showed their interest.

'How does it feel to be in the city after living several months in primitive areas?' was the first question they asked.

'Great!' we told them.

"Then they asked, 'Did you have trouble finding food?'

'No. There were all kinds of game and fish, plus the fruit and yuca we bartered for from the Indians we visited. We also brought dehydrated foods to supplement our diet.'"

"Jay, if you'd spent all your money, how did you get home?" Margaret asked.

"We got jobs working on a freighter bound for the United States. Before we could move aboard, we had to find someone to take our raft. The policeman watching it had a relative who was happy to get it and everything in it."

"In two weeks, the freighter was ready to sail. The night before we left, we got José to take us to see his father and thank him again for his thoughtfulness. At dawn the *San Francisco* left Belém. Our tears flowed as we recalled the help people had given to us, the kindness shown, the honors bestowed, and the marvelous time at the party. Not one of us would have dared to believe our adventure would end in such a stupendous way. At times it had looked doubtful."

Jay glanced around the room at his avid listeners. "I've attempted to tell you in one evening, about an adventure that lasted several months and involved people on two continents. Thanks for the opportunity to share it with you."

Mrs. Page asked, "Why didn't you go to Cuzco, Peru, where your parents lived?"

Jay grinned, then said, "I didn't want to miss out on the experience of working my way to Seattle with John and Paul. After we arrived, I called my parents and they sent me the money to fly down to Cuzco."

"Thanks, Jay," said every member of the Page family.

Margaret said, "Don't forget, Jay, I'm taking you to the airport tomorrow."

"I know. Let's get there early and we can have breakfast together."

It was time for Margaret to take him to the boarding-house. As he kissed her good night, he said, "Be careful driving home, and I'll see you in the morning."

Back in his room he reviewed the events of the day and how much he had enjoyed spending time with Margaret and her family.

As he waited for Margaret to arrive the next morning, he recalled the first day he saw her and how Russ had teased him. Even if he had been impressed when he looked into her dark eyes, never in his wildest dreams did he believe he could learn to care so deeply for her. His feelings differed from how he had felt about other girls. Although there had been attractive women in his life before, he kept each of them as friends, except Susan and Antonita. It had taken him years to forget Susan, and he now found Antonita in his thoughts less often.

He looked out to see Margaret waiting. Grabbing his luggage, he hurried to join her. Kissing her good morning, he said, "I"m going to miss you."

"Me too," said Margaret.

En route to the airport, Jay said, "You know I love you, don't you?"

"Yes, I believe you do, but we can't get serious."

"Why not?"

"I still have a year left in college, and you want to return to South America."

"I'd work to get established in my own company and then I'd come back for you."

"This is no time to get serious, though I do care for you."

"Passengers going to Canon City, the plane is ready for boarding."

Jay rose, took Margaret in his arms and told her, "It's tough leaving you. If God wills, I think some day you'll be my wife."

He held her in a tight embrace for a moment, kissed her, and hurried to board the plane. He looked back and saw Margaret waving to him. Perhaps she did care for him as much as he cared for her. He would have to wait and see.

# CHAPTER NINE

After Jay boarded the plane and found a window seat, he reflected on the difference between this flight—going for a job interview—and the flight leaving South America. To lose everything he had worked years for, even his heavy construction equipment, hurt. Though several months had passed, he was still troubled whenever the memory of what happened flashed across his mind. Then he recalled his father's words when he lost several thousand dollars in a bank failure. "Son, God has never left us nor let us go hungry. He will help us find a way to survive, perhaps better than before."

The longer he thought about his situation, he had to agree that some good things had come to him. Healthwise, he felt great since his surgery and stay in the hospital. Even though he lost Antonita, he had found Margaret. During this period when he was becoming accustomed to life in the United States, he'd told Margaret, "You're an inspiration to me and I thank God for putting you in my life."

She had smiled and said, "Thank, you, Jay. You're the same for me." Putting his thoughts aside, he glanced out the window.

The man sitting next to him said, "I enjoy flying when I can see great distances."

"So do I. I forget everything and concentrate on the plane's performance."

"Are you a pilot?"

"Yes. I have a year's air force and South American pilot's license. If I decide to stay in this country, I'll apply for an American pilot's license, too."

"By the way, my name is Carl James. I'm returning to my home in Canon City."

"I'm Jay Ryan, a civil engineer. I'm going to Canon City for a job interview."

"I work for the water department in Canon City. Presently, we're having problems."

"What's the difficulty?"

"Our department supervisor seems to think you can get water to run up hill."

Jay laughed. "I can tell you about a similar experience of mine. My dad decided to divert a creek to bring water to a house and barn. This was on our ranch in the foothills of the Andes Mountains. I idolized him and tried to do everything he did.

"I had watched men, under his supervision, dig the ditch and build a dam. So, I dug mine and made a dam at the opposite end and waited for the water to flow. Nothing happened. I went over and looked at the ditch the men had dug. Water flowed in from the creek. I dug mine deeper and watched, but the water stayed in the creek.

"When Dad came home that night and asked me how my project turned out, I told him about the trouble I had trying to get water. He promised to look at it next day.

"I'll never forget the grin on his face when he saw my ditch that morning. He was a tall man, over six feet, and I was a short five-year-old. I looked up at him, waiting to hear what he would suggest. Finally, he stepped back, put his arm around me, and said, 'Son, water won't flow up hill.'

As the two talked, a puff of dark smoke billowed from the left engine. Jay gasped and said, "Oh, no!"

"What's wrong?" Carl asked.

"Nothing serious I hope. The smoke reminded me of when I was a member of a scientific expedition into the jungle in South America. All our supplies and equipment were freighted by railroad to an airport located at 13,000 feet in the Andes Mountains. From there, the expedition hired a three-engine plane called *Condor.* It was equipped to haul freight at high altitudes. After leaving the airport, we had to climb to 17,000 feet to clear the last high peaks before beginning to descend into the forest lands.

"We'd already made several flights to the expedition's jungle headquarters. Taking off from the airport and coming up to the snow peaks, we had to line up with a pass through a turbulent area. It rocked our plane like a ship in a rough sea. Once we left the pass, it was smooth flying."

"What was the purpose of the expedition?"

"To map the forests of the different countries that owned the land. Since we were in a part that was inhabited by primitive tribes, they sent soldiers along to protect us.

"Our expedition headquarters were in a hotel near the airport. When we left, after three months, they presented us with a huge basket of food for our lunch, as a farewell gift.

"Things went well during the flight, until we began to descend. Then smoke poured from the left engine before it backfired and stopped."

"I'll bet your heart came up in your throat fearing what might happen."

"Yes, and it got no better. The engine smoked worse and they shut it down. We'd barely traveled one-quarter of the distance and were at a point of no return."

"Now that's scary," said Carl.

"The expedition chief left the cockpit and came to join Jim, an engineer, and me.

'If we can't land on a river beach, we'll crash on the heavy trees,' he said, before going back up front.

While Jim and I shifted cargo around to better balance the plane, we found the lunch gift.

'Let's keep up our strength,' I said, taking a sandwich and passing one to him.

"We'd no sooner gulped down our food, when I realized the plane was losing altitude fast.

'Let's crawl back into the tail section before the plane crashes.'

"As we braced ouselves, we felt a rough bump followed by two more. We were on the ground! We scurried through the fuselage to the door and jumped down to find the crew and the expedition chief inspecting the plane.

"Looking up, the chief told us, 'Surely a Higher Power helped us land without the plane catching fire.'

'Yes,' said Jim, 'He sure did.'

"I said, 'Thank you, Lord.'

"Well, so goes the adventurous life of a pilot over South America."

"Whew!" Carl whistled. "In my imagination, I could feel the plane losing altitude and getting ready to crash."

"We were fortunate it didn't."

"I've enjoyed talking with you, Jay, and hope I see you again. Here's my business card.

When you know the results of your interview, give me a call. I'd like to invite you to my home to meet my wife and sons."

"Thanks, I'll let you know how it turns out. It's been a pleasure talking with you and I'm looking forward to seeing you again and meeting your family."

Their conversation was interrupted by the captain reporting, "We will be landing in fifteen minutes. Please fasten your seat belts."

The stewardess checked all rows then took the last seat and fastened her belt.

As the plane touched down, someone sitting behind Jay, said, "We're back where we started. What happened?"

The stewardess explained, "When the trouble with the left engine began, we were nearer to this airport. It was better to return and transfer all of you to another plane."

The passengers filed into the airport to wait for the next plane. Carl James called his supervisor to report the delay and was given a new assignment. He looked for Jay. Finding him, he said,"I was hoping to hear more of your stories, but I have to stay over. Have a safe trip and be sure to call me."

"Sorry you can't make it, Carl. I'll let you know the results of the interview."

125

He hurried to a phone booth and called Trevor Price, the personnel manager of the Diamon Construction Company, to explain the delay.

"No problem," Trevor assured him. "We'll have someone meet you at the airport whenever you arrive."

He went into the restaurant, ordered a cup of coffee, and watched the planes. An attractive young lady hurrying to make her flight, reminded him of Margaret.

It was growing late, the shadows were lengthening and the plane supposed to take him to Canon City had not shown up yet. He began pacing back and forth. Was this God's way of telling him not to take the job? He watched a plane come in for a landing.

Going over to the airline desk, he asked, "Is this the plane to Canon City?"

"Yes. You can board anytime. It leaves in 20 minutes."

He joined the other passengers walking down the ramp. Soon after he fastened his seat belt, the plane left the runway and they became airborne.

Glancing at the scene below, he saw fields covering the low rolling hills and level patches of land turning the countryside into a quilt of lovely earth colors.

"It's fantastic the way those plots of stubble and plowed ground form a pleasing design," said a man across the aisle.

"It's unbelievable how attractive it is from this aerial viewpoint," Jay told him.

The two chatted a short while, then the man leaned back and dozed. Jay stared out the window, recalling the months he'd spent in the hospital. It was during that period, when his future looked bleak, that he doubted he would recover and work on a challenging engineering job again. Thanks to God and skilled medical help, he was as strong and healthy as ever.

Enjoying the flight, his thoughts were interrupted by a voice over the loud speaker that announced, "We will be arriving at the Canon City airport in approximately fifteen minutes. Secure your seat belts."

After the plane landed and Jay came inside the terminal, a young man approached and said, "Pardon me, are you, Jay Ryan?"

"Yes, I am."

"Good! I'm Richard Knox. I work for the Diamon Construction Company. Now that you're here, let's get your luggage and I'll take you to your hotel."

When they'd reached the hotel, Richard said, "At 7:45 A.M., someone will come take you to the main office."

"Thanks, I'll be ready," Jay said.

Once in his room, he dropped into the nearest comfortable chair, closed his eyes, and rested a moment. It had been a long day and he was tired. Later, as he got into bed, he was grateful for the hotel's location. The quiet street made it easier for him to relax and go to sleep.

The next morning he reviewed his résumé notes and sought God's guidance for his life before going to breakfast. Soon after he entered the dining area a man came over to his table.

"Good morning, Jay, I'm Trevor Price," he said, extending his hand.

"Nice to see you," said Jay, rising and shaking hands with him. "Please join me for breakfast."

"Thanks, I will," he said, drawing up a chair.

"Good morning," Trevor said to the waitress, "I'd like ham, one poached egg, whole wheat toast, some orange juice, and coffee." Turning to Jay, he said, "I eat a hearty breakfast when I have a busy day ahead."

After eating, Trevor took him to the main office to meet the chief engineer.

"Mr. Wood, this is Jay Ryan and here are his papers."

"Thank you, Trevor. Please put them on my desk."

Trevor placed the papers in a neat stack and left the room, closing the door behind him.

"Well, Jay, I see you've made it. We were a bit concerned yesterday."

"Airplanes are great until there's trouble, then it's a different story."

With a laugh, Mr. Wood said, "How well do I know it. Last week we made an unplanned landing when the company plane developed mechanical problems soon after we became airborne. Fortunately, we made it back to the airport and got the problem solved."

"Do you fly?" Jay asked.

"Yes, and I see by your résumé that I have a veteran pilot in front of me."

"Just a pilot, sir," Jay answered.

Mr. Wood glanced again at the résumé, then began asking technical questions pertaining to engineering. The interrogation continued throughout most of the morning. As hours passed, he leaned forward, listening intently to Jay's answers.

When there were no more questions, he said, "Take the afternoon to look around. Tomorrow we'll visit the site where we plan to build the road. I'll stop by the hotel for you at seven A.M."

"Before I go, may I have a set of specifications and drawings of the project?"

"Sure. Miss Hendricks, please get a set for Mr. Ryan."

She returned shortly and gave the plans to Jay.

Jay smiled and said, "To be getting back into engineering gives me a good feeling."

"I can see you'll have little time to tour the city this afternoon. If you prefer, I can take you to your hotel on the way to my meeting with the city council."

"Thanks. I hope it's not out of your way."

"No bother at all," he said.

Back at the hotel, Jay ate lunch then went to his room. He slipped off his suit jacket, loosened his tie, and looked over the project plans. He became so engrossed in studying them, he worked long past the dinner hour. But his study had shown him what he needed to know and how he could use the information.

He put away the plans and leaned back in his chair, reflecting on what a difference the day had made in his life. He had spent such concentrated effort studying the papers all afternoon, he was sure he would dream about the project, even before he had been to the site.

# CHAPTER TEN

He awoke early, ate breakfast and waited for Tom Wood to arrive. When he parked in front, Jay hurried out with the project papers under his arm.

As he got into the car, Tom said, "We'll travel by company plane to the site. There's a small landing strip on a farm near another project. We're building a dam across the South Platte River to provide irrigation. Without water, the land won't grow anything."

"Is it far to where we're going?" Jay asked.

"It's 230 miles and will take us about an hour to get there."

"How does stormy weather affect traveling to the job?"

"We avoid bad weather by beginning our work in early spring and shutting down as winter approaches. How did you do with the drawings and specifications yesterday?"

"I see the timetable fits in with what you've told me. By the end of October it should be finished and accepted."

"Raymond Homer, our project engineer for the dam, will meet us at the landing strip. He lives in Camaron. The proposed ski lodge sits 14,380 feet above sea level and is one mile west of Woodland Park. To reach it, we have to build four and eight-tenths miles of road. It'll be quite a contrast from some you've worked on or seen. I remember reading about an engineering project in South America where the railroad begins at sixty feet above sea level. Trains using the track to cross the continental divide reach an elevation of over 14,000 feet above sea level, four hours later."

Jay smiled and said, "I've ridden that train several times. There's a tunnel over seven miles long. It has three switchbacks and two complete circles of 180 degrees for turnarounds inside mountains of solid rock. In one place a river was diverted to use 300 yards of riverbed for building the track. An American engineer designed and built the railroad. It's considered one of the engineering marvels of the world."

"I'd like to take a trip across the continental divide," said Tom, as he circled the plane to see if the landing strip was clear.

"No livestock grazing today, so down we go," he said, making a steep dive.

"A perfect three-point landing, Tom," Jay said after the plane touched down.

"Not bad," Tom said as he taxied to a parking place. After he climbed down, he asked Jay to bring their lunch.

Expecting a light-weight bag, Jay had to lean to one side when he picked it up.

He said, "You must be planning an extended stay."

"No, it's the kind my wife packs when I'm out in the field."

Glancing around, Tom said, "We picked a good day for our visit."

"Perfect," said Jay.

"And," said Tom, "so is our timing. There's Raymond with the jeep."

Raymond parked and came to meet them. After Tom made the introductions and they talked, he said, "Raymond, we know you need to get back to the water project, so let's stop by your office and let you out. Then Jay and I can take the jeep and go over to the road project. We'll return in time for you to take us to the plane."

As they drove, Jay observed that Tom was not only a good pilot, but also a skilled driver. Although the center line was well marked, there was barely room for cars and trucks to pass by as they met each other, as shown by the work of a surveying crew.

At the site, Tom locked the jeep and reminded Jay, "If we're going to get back by two o'clock for lunch, we'd better get started."

Concentrating on the work, they lost track of time. It was a quarter past two when they returned to the parked jeep.

Until Tom began unpacking a mountain of food, Jay had not thought about it. Yet with all the walking he had done, he had worked up quite an appetite.

While they were eating, he said, "Man, this hits the spot!"

"Yeah, the physical exertion does this to us. Soon as we finish eating, we'll leave so you can see where our engineers stay."

As Tom drove, he mentioned points of interest and shared bits of information about the town and what it had to offer. Soon he left the business district and went to a new residential area. "I want you to see the apartment we reserved for the project engineer taking this job," he said.

Jay liked everything about it from the new appliances in the efficiency kitchen to the two bedrooms. The master bedroom looked out on a gorgeous rose garden.

"Wow! It's late," said Tom. "We've gotta hurry so Raymond can get us to the plane. When we're airborne, I'll fly over the project to give you an aerial view."

"Thanks," said Jay.

Raymond was waiting when they arrived. En route to the plane, Jay told him, "I'm sorry there's been no time for me to see your project."

"There's never enough time," said Tom. "How's it going?"

"We're making progress and we're ahead of schedule."

"Those are the words I like to hear, Raymond."

At the landing strip, Raymond waited until they became airborne before he left.

Tom circled the project twice to give Jay the aerial view, then turned toward Canon City. He called a company employee on the radio and said, "We'll arrive at the airport by seven. Please meet us there."

Jay relaxed and fell asleep. He slept a short while before Tom woke him.

"How about taking over and letting me sleep?"

"Okay. First, please indicate bearing, altitude, cruising speed, location of controls, and when to wake you up to make the approach and landing."

Tom showed him what he needed to know, then dropped off to sleep.

After such a long absence, what a pleasure it was to have his hands at the controls of a plane. He glanced at Tom comfortably snoozing and thought, he is as weary as I am and eager to get home.

Enjoying the smooth ride, he was startled when the plane made a different sound. He checked everything, but found nothing wrong. Then he heard it again and decided he had better wake Tom.

The instant Tom heard it, he said, "That's the same problem we had when we turned back and landed at the airport. Let me figure out where we are. If we're closer to the project, that's where we'd better try to land."

Tom alerted the control tower in Canon City. Then he called Raymond over the radio telling him to meet them at the landing strip. By the time they landed, the plane sounded like it was falling apart.

Tom contacted the main office in Canon City to report the trouble with the plane. He told them to get the Air Craft Maintenance and Repair Company to fly the next day to the landing strip to take care of the problem. He would activate the plane's beeper to guide them over and stay at the radio until they arrived.

Raymond was waiting to take them to a motel in Camaron. Both Tom and Jay were exhausted from the walking they had done plus tension resulting from the malfunction of the plane.

As they ate breakfast at 5:30 the next morning, Tom said, "With time to spare, we'll wait until we're back in the office to talk business."

Raymond took them to the landing strip. At eleven A.M., the service plane arrived from Canon City. The mechanics went to work and within a few hours they performed a flight test and said it was ready to resume regular work.

Tom and Jay finally left in the plane, followed by the service plane. They kept in contact by radio until they reached the airport in Canon City. As they taxied to the hangar, a man was waiting for them.

At the hotel, Tom said, "Get a night's rest, Jay. Tomorrow you'll be on the firing line."

Jay knew what he meant. He had to prove his capability before the job was his. His answers to tough interview questions would help Tom decide if he should recommend that the company hire him.

Jay drank a large glass of milk, showered, and fell into bed. He woke when the alarm sounded at four A.M. He reviewed the notes he had made at the project and felt prepared for any interview questions Tom might ask.

At 7:45 A.M. a car came to take him to Tom Wood's office.

As he entered, Tom said, "Let's sit where there's space to spread out the project drawing and specifications. Jay, I'll be asking questions that call for honest answers. After the interview, I must be convinced that you're the engineer we need for the project. I have to be sure before I present you to our general manager. Do you understand?"

"Yes, and I'll answer your questions to the best of my knowledge."

Tom closed the lengthy interview after he received satisfactory answers to all his questions. He acted convinced that Jay was the engineer for the project. He had training, experience, and credibility.

"It's time to meet John Wilmington, our general manager." He pressed a button at his desk and his secretary came.

"Miss Hendricks, please rewind the tape and take it to the general manager. I want him to hear it before I take Jay to meet him.

"That will be your tape to keep, Jay, unless you want it in your employee records, should you work for us. Let's discuss wages, benefits, expenses, and salary."

They had arrived at a mutually satisfactory agreement when the door opened and John Wilmington walked in.

"You must be Jay Ryan."

"Yes, sir."

"I've listened to your tape. Sounds like you're the project engineer for the job."

"Tom, I agree with your recommendation to hire him. Work out the details to make him an employee."

"Glad to have you with us, Jay."

"Thanks, Mr. Wilmington. I'm looking forward to working on this challenging job."

When Jay went for his medical examination with the company doctor, he felt confident of passing it. Upon seeing the massive scars left from his war wounds, however, the doctor called Tom and recommended that Jay be examined by the doctors in the hospital where he was last treated. Their report should be final.

Acting upon the doctor's advice, the company made arrangements for Jay to fly to the hospital in Grand Junction the following morning.

Back in the hotel, Jay reviewed how this unforeseen happenstance had abruptly altered his plans and could affect his future. He struggled to remain calm and analyze his situation. He found it difficult to put the issue in its proper perspective.

He decided to call Margaret.

"Tomorrow I'll be flying out to the hospital in Grand Junction for an examination by the doctors who treated me. The company needs to know if I'm in shape to handle the job."

"Jay, I'm sorry. I wish there was something I could do to help you."

"Then call and ask the hospital when visiting hours are and come see me."

"What if they won't let me?"

"I think they will, at least give it a try."

"I will, Jay."

"Good. If I get the job, this may be my only chance to see you for a long time. I am supposed to leave after the tests are completed and report to the company at Canon City."

"I'll try to make it, Jay."

After Jay finished talking with Margaret, he planned to go to bed early and get his rest. Then he remembered his promise to Carl James regarding the interview results.

He called Carl's home. "This is Jay Ryan. May I please speak with Carl?"

"I'm sorry, Mr. Ryan, he isn't home. Please leave your phone number and I'll have him call you when he arrives."

A half hour later the phone rang. It was Carl.

"I'll be at the hotel in twenty minutes. I want you to come to dinner."

"Carl, I hope I'm not imposing."

"I've told Ann and the boys about you and they're looking forward to meeting you. So, I'd better stop talking and leave for your hotel."

At the hotel, Carl asked, "How did the interview go?"

"It went well, but I have to return to the hospital for an examination by the doctors who last treated me. "

"You won't have any trouble passing your physical, Jay. You really look healthy." They chatted as they drove along and in a short while Carl pulled into a driveway.

"Here we are, Jay."

Carl's wife, with two young boys beside her, greeted them. "Jay, this is Ann, and these are our sons, Jeffrey, eight, and Stephen, six."

"Nice meeting you. I'm honored to be in your home," Jay said, smiling.

"A pleasure to have you. Wish I could recall the Spanish welcome."

"You mean, "Mi casa es su casa?""

"Yes. It's the neatest way of saying, 'Make yourself at home.'"

Stephen looked at Carl and asked, "Dad, is this the real Mr. Jay Ryan?"

"Yes, he's the man I've been telling you about."

Ann said, "If you'll excuse me, I'll get dinner ready to serve."

At the table Jay sat between the boys who treated him like a celebrity or a favorite uncle. It was great to be a guest in their home. A caring family, they enjoyed their own and other's company.

Later in the living room, Carl said, "It's fantastic how well your interview turned out."

"It's been such a long while since I've worked, I can hardly believe it myself."

"Jay, the boys want you to tell about your childhood in South America," said Ann.

"I'll have time for one story before I go to the hotel. I went to South America with my parents when I was two years old. At age six, they enrolled me in a mission school, which was so far from our house, I had to stay there all week.

"Then we moved to a large ranch in the Andes Mountains. There I rode my pony, Cayuse, to visit my Inca Indian friends at the village on our ranch. On the way I got to see where the giant condors built their nests up on the high cliffs. Juan, our foreman, let me ride with him to check our cattle. Once he let me go cougar hunting with him, but that's another story, I'll tell you someday."

"What's a cougar?" Stephen asked.

"A magnificient-looking animal, like a lion."

"Did you have towns where you lived?" asked Jeffrey.

"It was two days on horseback from our ranch to town. We traveled over narrow trails winding past blue glaciers where the ice never melted. We had to carry our food, grain for the horses, sleeping bags, and warm clothing for when we rode along a trail at 15,000 feet elevation.

Glancing at his watch, Jay, said, "I'm sorry to trouble you, Carl, but could you take me to the hotel? Thanks for inviting me to your home and for the delicious dinner."

"It's been a pleasure, Jay. Wish you could stay longer."

At the hotel, Jay said, "Your family is precious. I'm glad I got to meet them."

"So am I."

He hopped out and waved before going inside.

# CHAPTER ELEVEN

Back in his hotel room, Jay packed his luggage in readiness for leaving the next day. Tom Wood had made arrangements for his transportation to the airport at seven A.M. as the plane to Grand Junction left at eight.

Before he left the office, Tom told him "Don't worry about getting to the hospital for your examination. When you arrive, they'll have someone waiting to take you there."

"Thanks, Tom."

"We like you, Jay. We hope things work out and you'll be back with us soon."

It was late when he hopped into bed. Too excited to sleep, he reviewed the time spent with the James family. Who would have dreamed a friendship could develop from a chance encounter on a plane trip? Who would have imagined the girl he met, a staff member of the Grand Junction library, would take his heart? He reflected on how chance encounters had influenced his life, like being in the right place at the right time. That's how he had met Margaret. Thinking of her and what she meant to him, helped him relax and fall asleep.

He awoke early, dressed, and hurried down to breakfast. He barely finished eating when a car from the Diamon Construction Company stopped out front. The driver was the young man, Richard Knox, who had met his plane when he first arrived in Canon City.

Later, as the plane became airborne, Jay felt apprehensive about the pending examination. Although he was unaware of any health problems, one never knew what life-threatening disease lurked in his body, waiting to attack.

When the plane landed at the Grand Junction Airport, Jay hurried toward the terminal as he heard, "Jay Ryan, please report to the front desk," spoken over the loud speaker.

A hospital attendant met him midway and asked, "Are you Jay Ryan?"

"Yes, I am."

"Let's get your luggage and I'll take you to the hospital."

En route, the attendant asked "Have you been a patient here before?"

"Yes. I was hospitalized there twice, but this time it's different. I applied for a job and the company wants to be sure I'm in excellent physical condition."

"Well, you've come to the best place to find out," said the attendant, as he parked near the hospital entrance.

Inside, the admittance nurse recognized Jay and said, "We wondered how you were getting along after you left the hospital. You must not be doing too bad. You look great."

"Thanks. This is just a checkup to be sure I'm in good shape," Jay told her.

In a few minutes, he was assigned a private room with a telephone. As soon as he got into bed, he called Margaret at the library.

"Think you'll come see me tonight?"

"I don't know. I'll call and ask if you're allowed to have visitors."

"Please do. Remember, I'll be counting the minutes until I see you."

A half hour later, she called and said, "I'll drive over after dinner. Okay?"

"Perfect. I'll be waiting."

Jay cradled the receiver in his hand for a moment before replacing it. He felt happier since he had talked with Margaret. Though they had chatted for only a few minutes, it was enough encouragement to change his outlook on the future. Until he met her, it had never occurred to him that he needed someone in his life to love and cherish him. He had always been an independent person, perhaps too independent, he decided.

When the hour for visitors came, Jay was beside himself watching and waiting for Margaret. At last she came to his room, kissed him, and sat down in a chair by his bed. Clasping her hand in his, he said, "Margaret, now that you're here, I'm ready for the tests. I want to pass them and leave the hospital with a clean bill of health."

"I believe you'll do fine, Jay."

"I wish I'd met you before I lost everything. I would have had more to offer you."

"Perhaps it was just as well, Jay. We couldn't have married until I finished college anyway."

"Yeah, you're right, but it was a good thought," Jay said.

Visiting hours were over. As Margaret told him good-by, she held him close and said, "I'm wishing you the best. Call me before you leave for Canon City."

"I will. If I come through with no health problems and get the job, I'll write you each week, regardless of how busy I am."

"I'll be waiting to hear from you," Margaret said, then whispered, "I love you."

"And I love you," he said, kissing her tenderly and embracing her. "Drive carefully."

As she left, he said, "Remember me to your parents and brothers."

A nurse entering as Margaret left, said, "You surely had an attractive visitor."

"Thanks. I think so, too."

That night and the next two days took all Jay's time for the various examinations and tests the hospital administered. On the third morning, after breakfast, he was discharged from the hospital with a clean bill of health and the okay to work. An attendant took him to the airport.

While he waited for his flight, he called Margaret, to say things had gone well. He was heading for Canon City to work for the Diamon Construction Company.

As the plane became airborne, Jay reflected on how God had blessed him with a good health report, a new job, and Margaret. Her visit to the hospital had encouraged him.

Resolutely, he put aside his dreams of her and began to face reality. He thought about what responsibilities and challenges awaited him on the job. It was one of the biggest he had attempted in a long while. Yet he felt confident that Diamon had great trust in his capabilities, as project engineer for building the ski lodge road, or they would not have hired him.

He fell asleep and slept until the stewardess brought his lunch. He finished eating before they reached the Canon City airport.

As he entered the terminal, he saw Joe Barkley, assistant engineer, waiting for him.

"You have a room reserved at the hotel. While you're working in the main office, your transportation will be this rental car. Here are the keys. Get your luggage, go to the hotel and rest a bit. At three P.M., you and I will meet with Tom in his office."

"Thanks, Joe, I'll see you there."

It seemed like old times having a company car to drive. Not until he went to live in the boardinghouse, did he realize how inconvenient it was not to have one.

At the hotel, he went to his room. A few minutes before three, he walked into the main office. Tom's secretary, Miss Hendricks, greeted him.

"Good to see you. The chief engineer, assistant engineer, and general manager, are all waiting for you. Have a great meeting."

When he entered Tom's office, all three gave him a warm welcome.

John Wilmington, general manager, said, "I hope you're aware of the complications involved with this project. We're relying on your training and experience to make it a success, Jay. You'll be working with the chief engineer and his assistant. Once you three have outlined the procedures and requirements, we'll have a second meeting. Please tape record all your conversations."

The general manager left, and Tom Wood, chief engineer, said, "We've rented a furnished apartment for you in Camaron. It's the one you saw when we visited the site. We've hired a surveyor and his crew. They're ready to begin working with you."

"Could we have him spend tomorrow in the office with me?" Jay asked.

"I'll call and find out," said Tom.

Ten minutes later, he said, "Yes, he'll be here tomorrow at eight."

"To develop a plan of work for the company, I must spend some time at the project. We need to start staking with the required information to build the road."

"Great. I'll fly in everyone who needs to be there," said Tom.

The day spent in the office working with the surveyor was helpful. It gave them time to outline procedures to follow at the site.

Upon returning to the hotel that night, he called Carl James and said, "The hospital tests showed I'm in excellent physical condition. Isn't that marvelous?"

"It sure is. When did you get back?"

"Yesterday. I spent today working in the office."

"I'll come and get you, so you can have dinner with us."

"Thanks for inviting me, but you don't need to come get me. The company is letting me use a rental car while I'm working in the main office."

"Good. We'll expect you at 6:30. I'll tell Ann to set another place."

When Jay arrived, the family gave him a hug.

"Ann, did Carl share my good news with you and the boys?"

"Yes, he said the tests showed you're able to tackle a tough job."

As Ann called them to dinner, Jeffrey asked, "Are you going to tell us another story tonight?"

"I could, if you'd like to hear one."

"Let's hurry and eat so we can go to South America," said Jeffrey.

While they ate, Carl explained, "The boys have publicized your childhood in South America. One night last week we had a call from the school principal. He said the other students gather around the boys at recess to hear the stories they tell about Mr. Jay's personal experiences while living there. The principal said he would like to meet you and ask you to give a talk at school to all the students. Would you be willing to do it?"

"Sure, as long it doesn't interfere with my job."

Jay noticed the boys making signs to attract their parent's attention. They wanted to hear a story. Pushing his chair back, he said to Ann, "Thanks for the delicious meal."

After being excused, the boys took Jay by the hands and led him to the living room. Taking a comfortable chair, he sat down, and the boys sat on a small bench in front of him.

Ann called, "Don't start anything before we get there."

Carl and Ann soon came in and sat down. "Okay, we're ready for South America."

"Last time I told you about my parents' ranch up in the high Andes. This time I'll tell you how I learned to hunt when I was seven years old.

"My father was a skilled hunter and excellent marksman. Seeing how interested I was when he cleaned and oiled his guns, he ordered a small twenty-two, single shot rifle for me. When it came, I thought I was ready to use it. I watched while he unpacked it and stood waiting, my arms out ready to take the rifle. Holding it in his large hands, he showed me how to check to see if a rifle was loaded. He said, 'Always remember to do this check first thing.'

"Every morning for several days, Dad watched as I went through the mechanics of using the rifle. Then one morning, we walked to an area with grass and brush. He said, 'Let's see how well you remember what you've learned.'

"As I took the rifle, I became excited and almost forgot the most important safety rule until he said, 'Anytime you pick up a gun, always check to see if it's loaded.'

"I wasn't allowed to fire the first shot until I learned all of Dad's safety instructions. At last I qualified. Dad told me how to aim and when to fire at the target we set up. It was a four-foot-square, white board with a black dot in the center of a six-inch circle.

"I fired and the shot zoomed right past the large board. If it had been an elephant, Dad said he believed I would have missed.

"Later that day, I went to where he was working and asked, 'How big is an elephant?'

"He looked at me and asked, 'Why this interest in an elephant's size?'

'I want to know, because you said I couldn't hit one.'

'Son, I was referring to animals that must be six feet tall and fourteen feet long.'"

"Did you ever hit the little black dot in the center?" Jeffrey asked.

"Yes, I practiced every day for two weeks until I hit it five times out of five."

"Wow!" Jeffrey exclaimed, "You never missed."

"Now I'll tell you about my first hunt with the rifle. My parents went to the city and left me home in the care of our foreman, Juan, and his family.

"There were two Indian boys who took turns staying at our house. Evaristo, twelve, would stay a month, then leave so Serapio, eleven, could come. I learned to speak their Quechua language. Evaristo was at the ranch when my parents left for the city.

"One afternoon we saw a young buck grazing near the barn. Evaristo said, 'This is the third day I've seen him.'

"I said, 'Let's go hunting tomorrow at daybreak.'

"During the night, it rained, but at dawn the sky was clear. We slipped away from the house without telling anyone we were leaving and crept to where we saw the deer feeding. We crawled low to the ground, trying to get close enough before shooting. But each time we got close, the deer would run a few yards, stop and graze, then run again. This went on until he led us to the top of the hills, far away from the house.

"A heavy fog surrounded us, hiding everything. Walking into it was to disappear from view behind a thick curtain. Evaristo held my hand to help us stay together. We walked for hours without recognizing a familiar landmark. Meanwhile, the cold and dampness seeped through our thin cotton clothing and chilled us to the bone. My teeth were chattering and I had problems walking. I begged Evaristo to stop. He said, 'We can't stop. We must keep walking and find a warm place to sleep.'

"Shortly before dark, we came upon a potato field . 'There's a small cave nearby where my people stored the potatoes,' said Evaristo. We searched for the cave and finally found it."

Jeffrey asked, "Did you sleep in a cave?"

"Yes. We made a bed in the dry straw, lay down, and pulled some over us. Tired, we forgot our hunger and thirst and fell into a deep sleep. At dawn we looked out to see if the hills were clear of fog.

"Then we saw the deer. I fired, and he ran a few yards before falling. Just then we heard a dog bark. Forgetting the deer, we ran down the hill to the valley below and came upon an Indian hut. The family was ready to eat their breakfast of soup and baked potatoes. They were waiting for the woman's husband to come back with some fire wood.

"In Quechua, I told her, 'We're hungry. Would you give us some of your food?'

"Evaristo recognized the family as one that lived on our ranch and told her, 'This boy is the son of the owner.'

"She served us what was prepared and said she would cook more for the family. I told her they should get the deer we left upon the hill. When her husband came, his wife mentioned the deer and he left to get it. After we ate, we fell asleep.

"Late that afternoon, Juan rode up to the hut. 'Have you seen two lost boys?' he asked.

'Yes, they 're asleep in our hut,' the man told him.

"The instant Juan saw us, he said, 'You had everybody looking for you yesterday and today. Never leave the ranch without letting us know.'

"Ashamed of having caused so much trouble, I cried and said, 'Juan, I'm sorry. I promise never to do anything like this again.' Then I said, 'I shot a deer this morning, and we're having roast deer and baked potatoes. We want to stay tonight and rest.'

'Very well. I'll come in the morning and bring a horse for you boys to ride home.'

"That night after we ate, the family told fascinating stories until it was time to go to sleep.

Carl glanced at his sons and asked, "Boys, wasn't that a sad experience for a seven-year-old?"

"Yes, Dad," they agreed.

"Those are the kind of experiences," said Carl, "that help us learn how to survive in tough situations, even when we bring them on ourselves."

Jay said, "As we sneaked from the house, I felt quite smug with my rifle and had no idea the worry I'd cause others by not telling the cook where I was going.

"Carl, I'd like to meet the principal the first evening I return from the site. I'll tell the office to let you know when I'm coming."

"Wonderful. We'll be waiting for the call."

Thanks for everything," Jay said and left.

At the hotel, he assembled what he needed for work and got ready for bed.

He met Tom Wood in his office at seven the next day.

Tom explained, "The new four-wheel drive pickup we've assigned to you has a large tool box for your transit, level, and papers. It'll keep them dry and under lock and key."

"Just what I need," said Jay.

When Dick Jordan, the surveyor, and his crew arrived, everyone got into the station wagon and left for the airport.

# CHAPTER TWELVE

En route to the airport, Tom asked, "Jay, is your pilot's license current?"

"Yes," Jay replied. "I have my air force license and my license to fly in any South American country."

"Good. You'll pilot and I'll copilot for those times when I'm unavailable to fly."

"Can we circle the outskirts of town to help me locate landmarks for future flights?"

"No problem. Let's go," said Tom.

Jay contacted the control tower. "Requesting permission to take off and circle the outskirts of town at 1,000 feet before heading on our flight."

"Permission granted. Keep in radio contact with control tower."

Jay took off, circled the city, then headed for the project site. As they neared their destination, he asked, "Is there any kind of wind indicator at the landing strip?"

"No. Black smoke coming from the farmhouse chimney shows which direction the wind blows. A fire's always going as the family uses coal to generate heat and power."

"I see the smoke. I'll circle the field to check for livestock." After flying around it, Jay said, "It's clear, I'm going to land."

"There's Raymond and Harold with your new pickup."

When they landed, Tom said, "Raymond, I know you want to get back to work."

"Jay, while Dick and his crew look for reference points at the jobsite, you and I will drive to Camaron, get your apartment keys, and leave your luggage there."

As they returned to the plane later in the day, Tom said, "I'm pleased with the way you handle matters. Small details might not seem important, but they are the success of big things. You've put your heart into this project and you'll encourage those who work for you to do the same."

"Tom, rest assured, I will do my utmost to make it a success."

"The first time I saw you, Jay, I got the impression you were a professional I could depend on. The longer I know you, the more I'm convinced I was right."

"Thanks, Tom."

Jay waited until Tom left for Canon City, then drove his pickup to the project site. When he arrived, he joined the surveyor and his crew. They spent the day locating reference points and comparing their information with what was already in the reference point notebook.

Dick said, "It's hazardous walking over rolling pebbles and slippery grass. We need nylon rope to use as a safety line in the steep areas."

"We'll buy what we need this afternoon," said Jay.

"Tomorrow we'll eat breakfast at five and be at the job site by seven," he said to the crew.

After getting back to town and cleaning up, Raymond came over and they went to dinner.

"How's your project at the dam coming along?"

"Have a few problems to work out. The crushed rock from our quarry barely meets our specifications. I understand you might produce some crushed rock at your project."

"Yes. We'll have to see Tom when we put together costs for crushing."

"Tom told me you've spent several years in South America and graduated as a civil engineer from one of their top universities."

"Yes, I should be working for a company there now, but a few weeks prior to leaving for the job interview, the country issued some new regulations. In order to see what alternatives they might have, they closed down for a while. So, while I was waiting for them to solve their problem, I answered an ad Diamon Construction placed in a daily newspaper, and they hired me."

"I guess road constructon in those countries is tough," said Raymond.

"Building either roads or railroads there is a challenge. It's not uncommon to have a complete switchback or a 180-degree curve in a mountain tunnel. A river is sometimes diverted through a tunnel in order to use the riverbed for part of the road. Rivers are not only diverted for road beds, but also through a channel or tunnel to gain hundreds of meters in elevation to the proposed site for a hydroelectric plant. They use the tunnel as a tank to hold water and create pressure. You should plan to visit those countries,

Raymond. If I'm down there, I'll be glad to show you around."

Back in his apartment after dinner, Jay sat in his comfortable chair and thought of Margaret. He was shocked when he realized he had not written her since leaving Grand Junction. Where had the time gone, he asked himself as he prepared to call her.

When he explained why he had not written, she said, "I understand. With the long hours involved, you're no doubt working instead of writing. Why not call me?"

"Great idea, Margaret. What day should I call and when is the best time?"

"Saturday around nine P.M. would be perfect."

"Good. I'll call Saturday. You've no idea how I miss you."

"I know and I miss you, but as I told you earlier, we'll have to see how things work out after I graduate."

"You do love me, don't you?" Jay asked.

"Yes, but your heart is in South America. You'll take their first job offer and leave."

"We could get married and I'd take you with me."

"I'm not sure I want to leave my family and my country. Marriage is something very serious. We can't rush into it. Please try to be patient, Jay."

After Jay replaced the receiver, he thought, patience, I need it by the ton!

The next morning, he and his crew drove out to the site. Before they left that day, Jay walked the entire road project, making notes and taking pictures for reference.

On the evening of the third day, he asked Raymond, "Will you call Tom and have him arrange for someone to pick me up at the landing strip tomorrow at two P.M.?"

"Sure, no problem, Jay."

The following afternoon when Raymond and Jay reached the landing strip, Tom had landed and was waiting for them.

"How did things go at the project?" Tom asked.

"Good. It's coming along." Jay said.

"Raymond, before Jay and I leave, let's drive up to your project," Tom said, getting into the jeep. He had not visited it in several weeks and was pleased with the work done and what had been accomplished. Blue Rapids Dam was taking shape and looking good.

It was late when Raymond took them back to the plane and they left for the airport in Canon City.

Once they were airborne, Tom asked, "Now that you are familiar with the road project, what do you think of it?"

"It has potential for success. Tomorrow I'd like to discuss plans for developing it."

"Good. I'll be ready to start at 8:30," Tom said.

Jay piloted the plane to give Tom a chance to scan the notes Jay made at the site.

"Are they clear, Tom?"

"Yes. Even when you sometimes begin in Spanish and finish in English."

Glancing at an entry, Tom said, "I didn't know you had friends in Canon City or knew Carl James."

"I met Carl on my first flight to Canon City. He was my seatmate on the plane that developed engine trouble and turned back. I've visited his family, had dinner in their home, and shared stories of what it was like growing up in South America with their children, Jeffrey and Stephen."

Tom grinned and said, " How well do I know it. Ellen, our daughter, and Jeffrey are in the same classroom. According to her, the stories Carl's boys tell about Mr. Jay's experiences have made everybody curious to meet him. The school principal called me to get more information. They've even planned a one-hour assembly program for the students, teachers, parents, and invited guests. I'll be driving to this event with guest speaker, Mr. Jay," said Tom.

"Before I accept this speaking engagement, I want to be sure it doesn't interfere with my job."

"It won't, Jay."

"Thanks for understanding."

"I'll drop you off at the office. Your car is there. See you tomorrow."

"Thanks. Good night."

When Jay reached his hotel room, he called Carl James to say he was in town and hoped to see the school principal the next night.

"Can you come to the house tonight?" Carl asked.

"No. I have several things to put together for my meeting tomorrow at the office."

The following morning Jay met with Tom and his assistant, Joe Barkley, for their planning session.

Jay said, "Here's a list of things and equipment needed. If it doesn't compare with what you have, you'll know what extras we'll have to get. If we provide our own crushed rock for the road, about a mile from the project I've found a flat area large enough to develop a crushing plant and stockpile. Raymond mentioned he's not satisfied with the quality of crushed rock coming from his current pit."

"Work out a cost for rock, crushed and delivered to the dam, Jay. Joe will give you prices to use for equipment and mileage."

"If we crush, the drilling pattern will need to be changed to produce small rock, and we should know how much we'll need for both projects," Jay explained.

"Okay. We agree on the list of equipment you suggest. Work closely with our job coordinator, Jim Baker, a week in advance to be sure we meet your schedule. We'll start negotiating with the State for changing our rock source and increasing the unit price of crushed rock at the dam. Therefore, we must have your cost estimate as soon as possible. We also need to get an extension of time on your project. You'll find Ski Lodge Road, job 234, used on all correspondence. Raymond's project is South Platte River Blue Rapids Dam, job 222."

After lunch, Jay called Carl James. "Could I meet the principal at your house tonight at seven?"

"Yes. We'll be expecting you," said Carl.

When Jay arrived at the James' home, he found the principal, Mr. Andrews, waiting to see him.

After chatting a few minutes, he asked Jay, "What will be your subject?"

"Life with the Inca Indians of the Andes," Jay replied.

"It sounds interesting. Is Monday at one P.M. a convenient time for you?"

"Perfect. I'm looking forward to being in your school and addressing the students."

Mr. Andrews said, "You must've spent years in those countries; what's your opinion of their social class system?"

"They have three class divisions: lower, middle, and upper class. The lower class has a reputation for being honest and sincere. The middle class for being sincere. The upper class for being takers from the other two classes. In order to know them and what they're like, you need to live, work, and share with them. Learn to treat them with respect, whatever their circumstances or classification. For example, I had a construction company and kept all equipment in a storage yard. From the middle class, I hired a guard to watch the property. Items disappeared every week and he had no idea how or when they were taken. I dismissed him and hired one from the lower class. He and his family moved into the house vacated by the former guard.

"Being away from the storage yard days at a time, I never knew what to expect when I needed an item. It wasn't that way with the lower-class guard. Nothing was ever missing. I asked for an explanation. He smiled, then said, 'Very simple, Señor. I tell my friends if they steal anything, I lose my job and that keeps everybody honest.' Only by knowing them, can one make those kind of decisions."

"Jay, I'd like to talk with you longer, but I must go," said Mr. Andrews.

"Carl, I'd better go too, before I get involved in another midnight story," Jay said as he left.

Jay spent the next few days in the office with Jim Baker, working out costs on equipment, materials, and labor. Then he worked up the cost for job 234.

That evening after he returned to the hotel, he received a call from the principal.

"The students are ready and waiting for Mr. Jay. We'll see you Monday at one P.M."

"Thanks, I'll be there," said Jay.

At noon the following day, Tom came to Jay's desk, pulled up a chair, and sat down.

"Jim Andrews, the school principal just called. He's excited about the South American program on Monday. I assured him I would help Mr. Jay get there."

"Thanks, Tom."

"No need to thank me. Let's have lunch together."

"Great. I've worked up an appetite," said Jay.

Over lunch, Tom asked, "For as young as you are, how did you manage to live such an adventurous life?"

"Guess it's because I've looked for adventure in everything I did. The more dangerous and exciting the situation became, the more I felt challenged to do something about it. I was usually in the right place at the right time.

"Once while I was vacationing on a farm at the head of the jungle forest, Maxwell Stewart, an Englishman, stopped by. He was organizing an expedition to visit a claim owned by an English company. I told him I had to return to school in two weeks, but he said the expedition would only take that long, once we were organized.

"Soon afterward he recruited five men. I was the only one in this group with jungle experience or know-how to survive. Before we left, five others joined our team. Pablo Sanchez had spent much time in the jungle and he became the expedition chief.

"We were supposed to be in the holdngs owned by the English company. We set up camp and made racks for storing our things and sleeping. Then it poured rain for days and nights, flooding the area where we were. Hired packers failed to arrive with our supplies, even though we had cut a trail through the brush for them. We ran out of food.

"Pedro, the chief, said, 'We need a volunteer to go to the main headquarters base.'

"Without thinking of the danger, I stepped forward. After hugs from Pedro and the others, I left. It took over a day to make the trip. When I arrived, I sent the watchman at our main camp with a message to the store that had made arrangements to haul our supplies to the expedition's present location. I ate, rested a bit and started back carrying 60 pounds of supplies. I'll always remember what a good feeling it gave me to reach camp the next day with food for those starving men."

"Must not have been any game around," said Tom

"There was no game, no birds, no fish, nothing but water steadily rising. It was a dark moment for the expedition. Some members became delirious and had to be restrained. After it ended, Maxwell Stewart returned to England and wrote a book about his jungle experience. He must have mentioned me. Later, a group planning a scientific expedition to the jungles of South America read his book and contacted the American Embassy in Chile in search of me. They arranged my flight to the United States for an interview and a chance to join the expedition, which I did.

"Later, while I was attending college in Texas, two adventurous fellow students and I went to the headwaters of the Amazon, built a raft, and floated to the Atlantic Ocean."

The next morning, Tom called the state to report and make an appointment to meet with them in their office on Wednesday at ten A.M.

"You'll need to go with me, Jay. Ask Raymond to contact the state inspector and tell him of our intentions to propose crushing rock at job site 234 for job 222."

Jay spent the weekend working on his speech. He wanted to show the students how the Inca Indian parents on his father's ranch taught their children values to live by.

# CHAPTER THIRTEEN

Jay was shocked when he realized he had not written his grandfather since coming to work on the project. He sat down and wrote him a long letter. Then he wrote one to Enrique.

A glance at his watch reminded him it was time to call Margaret. After a lengthy chat, and then saying their good-bys, it was ten o'clock. Hearing her pleasant voice, even for a short while, had brought her near.

After he got into bed, he began thinking about his life on the ranch at the border between Bolivia and Peru. What happy memories came from his youth. One he cherished was listening to young Inca boys playing hauntingly beautiful music on handmade flutes, while their sheep flock grazed around them.

One day, after he was older, he asked his father, "Why did you buy this ranch?"

"Son, I wanted you to grow up in an environment where you could learn to relate to people without giving thought to their race, socioeconomic level, or cultural group."

Through his growing up years he had marveled at the way the Inca families had shown their liking and respect for his family. He did not understand why, until an elderly Inca man told him, 'Your father helps us, is kind, and treats us with respect.'

The longer he thought about it, the more he realized that was the way the Inca treated him and his family. He recalled the morning it began raining while he and Evaristo were far from the house. His cloth shirt offered no protection from the cold. Evaristo saw him shivering and removed his own water-proof shirt for Jay to wear.

"Evaristo," Jay cried, "without your shirt, you'll get sick!"

"No, I won't," Evaristo had assured him.

Thinking happy thoughts, Jay soon fell asleep.

When dawn came on Monday, Jay hopped out of bed, eager to begin the day. After he sought God's guidance and ate breakfast at the hotel, he left for the office and was the first to arrive. He worked until Tom came over to his desk, glanced at the clock, then said with a smile, "Mr. Jay, don't you think we should leave for the auditorium?"

"Yes. Thanks for the reminder, Tom."

Upon arrival, they found everyone seated and waiting for them. Mr. Andrews met them and escorted them to their front-row seat in the reserved section. Then the principal walked to the center of the stage and turned to face the audience.

"Welcome to this hour dedicated to our South American neighbors. Please rise and remain standing as our school band plays the national anthem. Then we will say the pledge of allegiance and be seated."

The honored student carrying the American Flag walked down the center aisle followed by fifteen students marching in perfect formation. Each student displayed the flag of a South American country. As the flags of all the countries in South America passed in review, everyone rose.

"Please remain standing at attention," said Mr. Andrews, the Master of Ceremonies. "As I call the name of a country, the person carrying the flag of that country will step forward and place it in its stand."

After all the flags were placed, he said, "Thank you, students for a fine job. Everyone please be seated.

"It is our privilege to have Mr. Jay Ryan as our guest speaker today. He is the son of American parents, and was born in Texas. At age two, he moved with his parents to South America. His first schooling was in an Anglo-American school where he studied Spanish in the morning and English in the afternoon. He received part of his university training in the United States and graduated as a civil engineer from a South American university in Chile.

"Before I bring him up here, I want to thank Mr. Tom Wood, Chief Engineer of Diamon Construction Company, for granting our speaker time away from his job to be with us today.

"It is my privilege to present to you, Mr. Jay Ryan."

"Thank you, Mr. Andrews. Now I want to thank two friends for their part in this hour of sharing. Jeffrey and Stephen James, please stand up. Let's give them a a big hand. Thank you, boys.

"Today I want to tell you what it's like to live among Inca Indians in the Andes. A thousand years ago the Inca had one of the most advanced civilizations in the world. They're most famous for the stone cities they built including Machu-Pichu up in the mountains. Some of the stone roads they built are still being used. The people I'll be telling you about have passed their language, history, and stories down through each generation to the present time.

"When I was five, my parents bought a ranch in Peru near the Bolivian border. Fifty Inca families lived in a village on our land, as had their ancestors generations earlier.

"This Inca community was made up of the elderly, widowed, middle-aged parents with grown children, and young couples with small families. Their officials were a governor and two captains who were elected every two years. The governor was in charge of the community and his decisons were final.

"The captains served under the governor, taking messages and visiting all the families. Whatever type of work needed to be done, whether building or repairing a house for someone, or planting a crop, they worked as a group.

"At planting time the governor and captains went to see the landlord, my father. They told him where they planned to prepare and plant corn at the lower elevation and potatoes at the higher elevation. The landlord would then approve their plans. The governor and captains laid out the land parcels with the landlord getting the largest, then the governor, elders, widows, captains, and finally the young families.

"The steep hillsides where they grew corn, pumpkin, squash, and beans had to be cleared of trees and brush. They cut trees halfway until they reach top of the hill, then they cut them through, so that all the limbs would break as the trees fell in sequence.

"Months later, when it's dry and there are strong winds, they set fire to the cut areas. This gets rid of bugs and weeds on the land the men have cleared. However, smoke from these fires darkens the sky for days and turns the sun into a giant gray ball.

"At harvest time, they use pack horses to deliver the crop to each family.

"One morning my parents saw the governor and captains stopping at our house. They wanted to know where to store the landlord's portion of everything that had been produced. This was my parents' first year on the ranch. No one had mentioned that the landlord was supposed to get a share. It was an Inca way of saying thanks for use of the land.

"Dad was surprised when he saw all they had brought. While he tried to think of a place to store it, the governor said, 'We've brought material and tools and will build a barn if you like.'

"Dad said, 'Thanks for your kindness.'

"While they worked, Dad learned that the governor had observed on a previous visit, that there was no storage facility, so the crew had come prepared to build one. The barn was finished and the produce inside away from the weather and animals before they left that day.

"My parents admired how the Incas cared for the elderly, widowed, and orphaned, and those who were unable to do their share of the work.

"As time passed, I learned their Quechua language. To practice, I chose two young boys to stay at the ranch with me. We treated them as family. One would stay a month, then return to the village to let the other one visit.

"A month before Christmas that first year, Dad had the governor and his captains come to our house. Dad told them he wanted to do something special for all those living on the ranch. It was to become a yearly event. Dad designated a large steer and six sheep for an open-pit barbecue. 'Take any produce we have on the farm to go with it,' he said. 'I want every man, woman, and child to attend this celebration.'

"We had a fantastic time that Christmas Day. Along with the barbecue, roast corn, baked potatoes, beans, and squash, Mother and the cook served all kinds of delicious cookies, cakes, and breads they had baked. Soon after we ate, Dad brought out two large bags of gifts. He and mother distributed them, and no one was forgotten.

"You know, if we treated others the way we would like to be treated, the world would be a better place. That's the way our Inca people of the High Andes lived. Thanks for giving me this opportunity to share."

Mr. Andrews, "Thanks for sharing your experiences with us."

En route to the office, Tom said, "I believe the students enjoyed the program as much as I did. Wonder if I could persuade Mr. Jay to be guest speaker at Rotary?"

"Yes, anytime, Tom. Would it be possible for us to fly to job 234 tomorrow? I need to check on the survey crew and equipment."

"Let me check my schedule," Tom said, flipping pages to a date. "No, I can't. You'll have to fly over yourself. Get back by four P.M. to have the plane serviced for our trip to see the state engineers on Wednesday."

"Early Tuesday morning, Jay left in the company plane for job 234. Raymond was waiting for him at the landing strip. Jay gave him the updated information on the rock crushing project that, hopefully, would be approved by the state on Wednesday.

"Thanks for the ride, Raymond. Please have your crew bus take the surveyor to the landing strip where I'll leave the pickup. I must be in Canon City by four P.M."

At the project, Jay found much work had been accomplished in getting equipment operators and maintenance crews on site.

The job superintendent, Douglas Turner, said, "I didn't expect to see you this soon."

"You've done well setting up camp. We want to keep it looking good," said Jay. "Has the surveying crew had problems with that steep section?"

"Not since we sent helpers to hold safety lines when they surveyed up there. It's so steep a mountain goat would rather go around than climb it."

Driving back to the plane, Jay could not believe how fast the hours had slipped by. He parked the pickup, got in the plane, and left for the Canon City airport. Upon arrival, he taxied down the runway to the service hangar and left the plane to be checked. He called Tom at his home and found everything was set for their meeting.

The next morning Tom said, "I've flown this route countless times, so I'll pilot."

Someone was waiting at the airport and took them to the engineering office of the state building.

Tom introduced Jay, "This is the project engineer for the ski lodge road."

After several hours of discussions and reviewing the plans and cost estimates, the state agreed to increase the unit price for crushed rock for the Blue Rapids Dam project

222 and extend the contract time by two months for project 234. Trails through open range, for moving supplies and equipment to the construction site, were to be graded back to their orignal slopes before project 234 could be accepted.

Tom thanked the people representing the State. On the return flight, he said, "This is great. We have a contract to crush rock for the dam, time extension for your project, and a better price for crushing rock."

"We can't begin crushing rock at the new site, until we know how many days it will take to dismantle the crusher, transport it and set it up. I should be at project 234 to discuss this change with the job superintendent and show him where to prepare the crushing site and access roads.

"Would it be possible to fly me there tomorrow so I can spend a few days and take care of these changes?" Jay asked.

"Yes, but I can't fly you over. Take the plane for a couple of days."

Early the next morning when Jay reached the landing strip, some cattle rested on part of the runway. Raymond chased them away and kept it clear until Jay landed.

Raymond said, "I have the answers to your questions."

That night Jay transferred the information Raymond had given him to sheets of paper for reference in his work with Tom later.

Friday morning he called Tom and said, "I'll arrive at the airport by five P.M. Things are coming along, but we're reaching the point where I should be here all the time."

When he returned to Canon City in the company plane, he found Tom waiting.

Back at the hotel, Jay ate dinner early and went to his room. He had not realized how weary he was until he plopped down to read the daily newspaper and fell asleep.

At ten on Saturday morning he awoke, dressed, and went to breakfast. He spent the day resting and reviewing the information he would present to Tom in the office on Monday.

Saturday night, as was his custom, he called Margaret at nine o'clock.

As soon as she answered, Jay, asked, "How's my precious sweetheart?"

"Good. Had a busy week at school and the library. How was yours?"

"Gave a talk to some students at an elementary school. Took a trip with the chief engineer to confer with the state people, and spent some time at the project site. I'll be moving to my apartment in Camaron soon and live there until the project's completed."

"Are you getting sufficient rest, Jay? Remember this is the first physical work you've done since you left the hospital. It may take time to build up your strength."

"I'm doing everything I can to get in shape."

"The library staff said they hoped things were going well on your new job."

"Tell them thanks."

"Margaret, you've no idea how I look forward to these calls each week. Our talks encourage me to keep working toward making you my beloved wife someday."

"You'll be interested to hear this, Jay. Not long ago, I asked my parents what they would think if you should ask me to marry you. Can you guess what they told me?"

"No, but I would hope they'd be pleased with your choice of a husband and accept me into the family."

"That's what they did. Dad said, 'Margaret, your mother and I discussed this possibility earlier. We would be happy for you and welcome Jay into the family.'"

"Marvelous! I'll do my utmost not to disappoint them or you."

"Think the boys would be willing to have me for their older brother?"

"What a question! They adore you."

"When we get married, we should include them in our wedding," said Jay.

"Oh, yes," Margaret agreed.

"I thought of a saying in Quechua: 'Chaska ñiwi sonko suwua.' In English it means, 'Eyes like stars and a thief of hearts.'"

"That's lovely, Jay."

"So are you. When I saw your beautiful eyes, you stole my heart."

"Why are we talking this seriously about wedding plans, when we can't marry for several months, maybe years?"

"It doesn't hurt to dream, for sometimes dreams turn to reality," Jay reminded her.

"You impulsive man, if you had your way, you would have us get married while you are working on this job."

"Right, then I'd take you to my apartment in Camaron. Nevertheless, it's as you say, we must have patience and wait. God will help us work things out and one day you'll be Mrs. Jay Ryan. Good-night, Precious. I love you."

"I love you, Jay. Take care of yourself."

The following weeks became demanding with everything at the project going full speed ahead. Though his strength was taxed to the limit, Jay enjoyed the work and seeing progress made, even if he fell into bed exhausted each night. He found he relaxed and slept well in his apartment, waking up eager to start the day.

Jay was disappointed that it took longer to dismantle and move the crusher to the new location, than he had anticipated. Then he had to get extra dump trucks to haul the crushed rock to the dam. As if that was not enough to slow their progress, after he told the drillers precisely how he wanted the holes spaced and drilled for explosives, they did not follow his instructions.

He called them together to explain the reason for the process, then showed how the job must be done to get the desired results.

One worker complained, "I don't see what difference it'll make if a hole's off a few inches."

"Trust me," Jay told him, "and do the work the way I've shown you."

Then he had a problem with Douglas Turner, the job superintendent.

"Jay, you college educated guys believe you know everything. Well, let me tell you something, I've been handling explosives in road building for years."

"Perhaps so, Douglas, but I'm interested in making a success of this project. I don't want anyone injured because of negligence or carelessness. My performance and safety record as project engineer has been good thus far and I want to keep it that way. When this road project is finished, I hope you can view it with a sense of pride and satisfaction, in what we've accomplished through cooperation and working together. If you have questions, or if I can help you, I'll be glad to do so."

He realized he must establish credibility with Douglas and the others. One way was to avoid asking them to do something he wasn't willing to do. If the possibility of danger existed in surveying a steep slope, he tied a rope around himself and worked with a mountain transit getting the needed information.

As days passed, Jay learned he had solved the problem with Douglas.

"While I'm working for you, Jay, your instructions are the law. I wanta learn from a professional who knows what he's doing and is willing to share his knowledge."

"Thanks, Douglas."

# CHAPTER FOURTEEN

After his conversation with Douglas, Jay saw he had proven his capability. Though the job was challenging, it was not as difficult as those he had worked on in the Andes, but he did not want to dwell on the past with its memories of what he had lost.

A few days later, Tom called and said, "I'll be coming to see how things are going."

"Great. I'm saving a surprise for you," said Jay.

The week passed. Tom got sick and sent his assistant, Joe Barkley, to check on the projects instead. Joe spent the first day at 234 and the second at 222. Pleased with the progress being made, Joe returned to the main office in Canon City.

Tom called Jay the next morning and said, "Got a good report from Joe on both projects. Jay, I've been trying to guess what your surprise is and I can't come up with anything."

"Then I'll tell you. We won't need the two-month's extension. The state inspector is amazed at the progress we're making on project 234."

"That's fantastic, considering how late we got started," said Tom.

A week later Tom called and said, "Meet me at the landing strip at ten A.M."

Jay arrived shortly before Tom landed.

He took him to the crushing plant where trucks were dumping blasted rock, loaders were feeding the crusher and conveyors to stockpiles, and a loader was filling trucks with crushed rock for the dam.

It pleased Tom to see progress being made, despite the occasional setbacks, and hear John Reed, the state inspector on the job, praise Jay's work. He chuckled at how John had complained, "I'm so busy I don't have time for a cup of coffee from my Thermos®. It's been a fast, smooth operation. One of the best."

"Glad you State Boys like how it's being handled," said Tom.

Later, Tom said, "Jay, whenever you have a contract with the government, as we do on this job, those who work for the owner, in this case the government, must see that the contractor complies with all their specifications in order to credit the good work they do. The contractor has no choice. He must accept their interpretaton of specifications. It takes someone like you, Jay, to set up the procedures for success."

Finished with his inspection, Tom called the office to say he was spending the night in Jay's apartment and would return the next day at four P.M. Then he asked Jay, "Are you still thinking about going to South America?"

"Yes. I'm committed to fly down for an interview with a South American company I was dealing with before I applied for this job."

"With your training and experience, you would be an asset to our company. I wish I could persuade you to stay. Is there another reason you want to go?"

"I want to visit my parents' graves in South America and pay my respects to them. They helped me become the kind of person I am today. Mother, a registered nurse, was my example of perfection in three areas: a loving mother, a devoted wife to Dad, and a helper to those in need. She was a strong woman. I saw her cry only once. It was the day she and Dad consented to let me take flying lessons. 'It's the most dangerous thing you can do!' she cried. Nevertheless, she agreed with Dad when he said, 'Who knows? In the future, it might be useful.'

"Dad, a capable engineer, shared his thoughts on simple and practical things in life. His example on principles in engineering created in me a sense of research, a desire to learn more about what he said. His patience in explaining answers to my many questions helped me decide I wanted to become a civil engineer."

"Jay, you had parents of whom you can be proud and I'm sure they must have been proud of you."

"Perhaps," said Jay. "They never knew what I might try to do next. I often acted impulsively and didn't take the time to think of the danger involved in the choices I made. Like when I was recovering from typhoid fever, I thought I could sneak a bite of steak with french fries and no one would know the difference, but I suffered a relapse. Mother said later it was a miracle I survived. After that, they really encouraged me to get the facts, think for myself, and consider the consequences of my decisions. It's been useful training."

At 2:30 P.M. Jay took Tom to the landing strip and waved as he became airborne.

The next few weeks kept Jay working and supervising to see that everything went according to schedule. Concentrating on various aspects of the job, he had almost reached the stage, where he could anticipate trouble and get the matter settled before things got worse and delayed progress.

Fortunately, the work crews took seriously his words regarding safety and no one got injured.

Working long days and falling into bed at night to get his much needed rest, kept Jay going and looking forward to the weekend and his Saturday night call to Margaret.

Once he asked, "Don't you think you should have an engagement ring, Margaret?"

"Yes, I like the idea, Jay."

When their conversation ended, he knew her ring size and the style she preferred. In his free time he visited jewelry stores looking for what she had described.

A few weeks later, Tom called. "Make arrangements to be gone two days. I'll be at the landing strip at 10:30 on Tuesday to pick you up."

"I'll be there," Jay said.

When Tuesday came, he was waiting in the pickup as Tom arrived.

"Didn't want to miss having you speak at the Rotary Club on Wednesday, Jay."

"I'll do my best, Tom. By the way, would it be possible for me to take off Thursday and Friday next week? I'd like to invite my fiancée to fly over and spend a couple days in

Canon City. She would be a house guest of Carl and Ann James."

"No problem, the project is going great. Finalize everything and let me know."

"I'll call tonight. If she does visit, I'll rent a plane and take her to see the project."

That afternoon Jay visited with office personnel and shared about some experiences gained. The general manager called him to his office.

"I've had excellent reports on your work. I also heard you're going to South America. I'd do anything to keep you, but Tom says you've decided to go. Do you expect to finish the job close to the original time?"

"Ahead of schedule, if everything goes well."

"That's encouraging. We'll see you at Rotary tomorrow."

On his way out, Jay stopped by Tom's office and said, "Thanks for all your help."

"My pleasure, Jay."

At the hotel, he called Margaret. Her father answered the phone.

"How soon do you expect her, Stan?"

"Any minute."

"I'll tell you what I have in mind. If she can fly over I'll have a round-trip ticket waiting at the airline desk in the airport. She will stay in the home of Carl and Ann James, friends of mine who live in Canon City. She's heard me mention them often. She told me she wanted to see my work. The ski lodge road project provides an excellent example."

"Here's Margaret, Jay. If she can go, you have my blessing."

"Thanks, Stan."

Margaret took the receiver and asked, "Jay, are you sick?"

"No. I'm calling to see if you can get away next Thursday and Friday to fly over to Canon City to spend the weekend. Ann and Carl James are looking forward to having you as their guest while you're here. On Friday you'll meet the office staff and on Saturday we'll fly to the project. Then on Sunday you can return to Grand Junction. If you can make it, I'll have a round-trip ticket waiting for you at the airport."

"I don't know. Depends on if Mrs. Hargrove lets me have the days off. If she gets the idea I'm coming to see you, she'll disapprove. If she asks, I'll say I'm visiting friends. What you've planned sounds fantastic, Jay. I hope I can make it."

"I'll be staying at the hotel tonight. Tomorrow I'll be the guest speaker at Rotary."

"Marvelous."

"I'll return to the project on Thursday and call you that night."

Jay called Carl and Ann James to tell them he had asked Margaret to fly over, but she had a few details to work out concerning being away from her job at the library. He would let them know if she could make the trip.

At Rotary the next day, Tom said, "It's my privilege to introduce the guest speaker, a civil engineering graduate of the University of Chile, who has lived and worked in all South American countries. I present Mr. Jay Ryan, a Diamon Construction Company project engineer."

"Thanks for giving me this opportunity to speak about those beautiful countries. The map will help you to understand the problems these countries face and their potential for developing their natural resources.

"Each country is special. Brazil, the largest and richest in natural resources, needs roads. Argentina, which is similar to the U.S. is beginning to develop its resources. Chile, between the Andes Mountains and the Pacific Ocean, produces some of the best fruit. Bolivia, with the highest airport in the world at 13,500 feet above sea level, also owns part of the highest navigable lake in the world, Lake Titicaca. Peru has three Andes Mountain ranges and Cuzco, the archeological capital of South America with all its museums and ruins of the Inca Indians, who ruled South American countries for over a thousand years.

"Now that I've briefed you on the geography, we can proceed with the questions."

"Who owns the other half of Lake Titicaca?"

"Peru."

"Does Bolivia have a port on the Pacific Ocean?"

"No, it has a treaty with Chile to use one of their ports without having to pay duty on goods to the country. Bolivia had, and may still have, a railroad into Chile. The grade was so steep that rails were made to fit sprocket wheels in the locomotives. My father told of a passenger train going on the railroad that sold first-class, second-class, and third-class tickets. A passenger bought a first-class ticket and sat down in the coach. When others entered carrying young animals and chickens and sat by him, he told the conductor, 'I must be in the wrong coach.'

"'No, you're in the right place,' said the conductor. Before long the train stopped. The conductor said, 'See the trail up the ridge? This train makes a switchback and will stop at the railroad station at the top. Passengers with first-class tickets remain seated; those with second-class tickets leave their belongings in the train, get out and walk to the station; and those with third-class-tickets leave their belongings in the train, go outside and wait. When the train starts to move, they push all the way to the top.'"

"Jay, we have requests for you to share an anecdote from your experiences while working there," said Tom.

"In a rugged, remote section where we were building a road, we found a level spot on top of a mountain. We managed to get two tractors up there. Then we bought ten donkeys and loaded each one with two five-gallon cans of fuel for the tractors. We put a can on each side of their back for balance. A man led them up a winding trail to the top.

"Upon arrival, their packs were removed and they were each given a sugar cube. When they came down carrying the empty cans, they were each given another sugar cube plus their feed. After a week's training, they knew the trail without being led and we had solved the problem of getting fuel up to operate the tractors."

"We have another question, Jay," said Tom.

"How would you describe the economy of those countries?"

"They are privileged because of all the natural resources they have. Yet they are underprivileged as they don't have the economics to develop them."

Afterward, Tom said, "You did great. What happened to the donkeys?"

"We gave them to the men who cared for them while we worked on the project."

As Tom and Jay returned from Rotary, John Wilmingon asked them to come to the office.

"Jay, the board of directors listened to a tape of Tom's report on your project and they're delighted with the results. They want you to stay with the company. The stockholders on the board would each transfer an equal number of shares to you, making you a stockholder, also. They voted to have this motion presented to you for your consideration."

"Thanks for your interest and concern. I'll keep it in mind."

Back in Tom's office, Jay said, "I need to check on the project. Can you fly me there tomorrow?"

"Meet me in the office at 7:30 and we'll be on our way," said Tom.

Later, in the hotel, Jay ate dinner and waited until it was time to call Margaret. She answered on the second ring.

"How did it go? Can you make it?"

"Yes, I can fly over."

"Good, I'll have the ticket for you at the desk in the airline office."

The next day, while flying to the job, Tom asked, "Will we get to meet Margaret?"

Smiling, Jay said, "On Friday. I can't wait for her plane to land at the airport."

Tom circled over the project and said ,"Sure looks good from the air."

"The Diamon Construction Company can be proud of their work," Jay told him.

Douglas Turner was waiting when Tom landed and let Jay out.

"I can't linger, Jay. I'll pick you up on Wednesday at four P.M."

"Thanks, I'll be here."

Jay worked hard the next week getting things ready so he could be away.

Finally, Wednesday came, when Tom was to pick him up and take him to Canon City. Everything was going well on the job and he found himself praying nothing would happen to prevent him from getting to meet Margaret's plane.

Though he stayed busy, time dragged and he thought 3:30 would never come so Douglas could take him to meet Tom at the landing strip. He had packed his dress clothes the previous night. He wanted to look his best for Margaret.

While he worked on some papers at his desk, Douglas came over and reminded him, "You said Tom was always early. Are you ready for me to take you to meet him?"

"Right, Douglas. Let's go. I'll be back early Monday morning."

They had barely parked, when Tom landed. Jay snatched his luggage from the pickup and waved to Douglas as he climbed into the plane. Tom sped down the runway ready for takeoff.

In flight Jay said, "I appreciate this kindness."

"Glad I could do it, Jay. Margaret sounds like a marvelous young lady."

"I think so, and I really care for her."

"While in town, Jay, the rental car is at the office for your transportation."

"Thanks, again, Tom."

That night, if Jay had not been so tired, he would have had difficulty sleeping. As it was, after he ate dinner, he went to bed and slept soundly until nine the next morning.

At 1:30 P.M. he left for the airport to meet Margaret's plane.

As soon as it landed, he hurried around the others, searching for her. They met midway. He took her in his arms and gave her a tender kiss.

"Have you missed me?" Margaret asked.

"What do you think?" he asked, kissing her again.

"Jay, I'd like to go some place where we can talk before you take me to meet Ann and Carl."

"Great," said Jay, his arm around her as they walked. "Let's get your luggage and go to the ice cream parlor."

While they filled each other in on what had happened since Jay left for the job, he said, "Tonight, I'm taking you to an elegant place for dinner where we can share our dreams and store up cherished memories."

"How thoughtful of you, Jay."

He glanced at his watch and said, "We'd better leave so I can take you to meet the James family. They're looking forward to having you as their guest."

At their home, Margaret got a warm welcome. Jay visited for an hour, then said he wanted to arrive early at the restaurant where he and Magaret were having dinner.

Back in his room at the hotel, he showered and dressed with care. Before he left to get Margaret, he opened the lid of the velvet-lined box containing her ring. He felt sure she would be pleased with its beauty. Closing the lid and putting the box in the pocket of his suit jacket, he left.

At the house he visited for a few minutes, then said, "We'd better go."

It was a pleasant drive to the restaurant. There, as they were seated at a table for two, soft music provided the mood and atmosphere Jay desired for the special occasion.

As dusk came on, he smiled, took Margaret's hand in his and said, "I love you and I believe you love me. The time has come for me to show how much I care for you and want you to be my wife."

"Yes, I love you too, Jay."

He took the small box from his pocket and opened it to reveal a brilliant diamond in the candle light.

"Margaret, this ring is a symbol of my love and commitment to you."

With all the love, admiration, and respect she held for Jay, her eyes grew misty and she said, "I love you with all my heart." Jay slipped the ring on her finger and kissed her.

As they sat close holding hands, Jay smiled and said, "I planned to give you the ring after dinner, but I couldn't wait that long."

"I'm glad you didn't. It's lovely. I can enjoy its beauty while we dine."

They lingered over the meal until Jay said, "It's been a long day and you're going to be on the go while you're here, so I'd better get you back and let you rest."

Jay drove with Margaret snuggled up against him until they reached the James' home. He kissed her good night and escorted her up the walk to the door where Ann waited.

"Have time to come in, Jay?"

"No thanks, Ann. I'll be back at ten tomorrow. I want to show Margaret around the area before I take her to lunch and to meet the office staff."

"Keep Friday night clear, so the two of you can have dinner with us at the house."

"Thanks, we'll do that."

As he drove to his hotel, Jay reviewed what happened and how he had committed his love and agreed to wait for Margaret until she graduated.

At the office on Friday afternoon, the staff served tasty refreshments. Jay thanked them and said he was glad Margaret got to meet everyone.

They left and spent the remainder of the afternoon sightseeing and discussing their future plans until Jay said, "We'd better get to Carl and Ann's for dinner."

As they rang the doorbell, Carl, said, "Sure glad you're here. Guess you know, Margaret, we highly regard Jay and the way he has made the arrangements for you to visit."

"I know, and I want to thank you two for giving me the opportunity to be a guest in your home. I've appreciated and enjoyed every minute," said Margaret. "Your boys are precious. They remind me of my brothers."

Jay stayed an hour longer, then left.

Soon after he got to his hotel room, the phone rang. It was Tom Wood.

"Jay, I told the general manager you planned to rent a plane to show Margaret the project. He said no need to rent when you could use the company plane."

"Wow! Thanks, Tom and thank him for me. I'll be careful."

Would Margaret be surprised the next day. Excited, he stayed awake a long while.

Everything worked out as he planned. After he stopped at the James' house to get Margaret, he said, "We're going to the airport."

On the way, Margaret said, "It's a perfect day to fly and see the project."

"It couldn't be better," Jay agreed after they arrived and parked. Pointing, he said, "There's the company plane."

"It's beautiful, Jay, but where's the pilot?"

Jay grinned and said, "You're looking at him."

"You can't be serious, Jay."

"Yes, Tom called last night and said the general manager gave me permission. I'll help you inside and we'll get airborne."

"What a pleasant surprise!" cried Margaret. "I can't wait to see the project."

As they flew, Jay described the way the wild and rugged area had appeared before they built the road and how they worked to keep its natural beauty. His pickup was at the landing strip and he got to show her his apartment before flying back to Canon City.

After having dinner during their last night together, they returned to the James' house.

The time for Margaret to leave came much too soon. As Jay held her in his arms telling her good-by at the airport, his voice choked.

He said, "I'll cherish these memories of our time together. God bless you, Precious."

"And God bless you, Jay. Please be careful and take care of yourself. You know I love you with all my heart."

He held her close until she left to board the plane, then he hurried outside to wave as the plane taxied down the runway before it became airborne.

That evening he visited Carl and Ann James to thank them for their kindness and to tell the boys a story he had promised earlier.

"When I was your age, Jeffery, I lived in a boarding-house in the mission where I attended school. The lady teacher was strict with the girls and I seldom got to talk with Louanne, my girlfriend. So, I made a "telephone" using two round cans with the bottom cut out, a plastic piece over the end, and a large spool of coarse thread. She kept one can and lowered the other from her upstairs window. I took the lowered can and walked as far as the spool of thread would allow, then I'd start talking.

"Once, while I was enjoying my conversation with Louanne, I stayed out too long. I shuddered to think what would have happened had I been caught scurrying to my room!

"It's been great visiting with you, but I'm flying back to work in the morning, so I'd better go," said Jay.

He worked hard to complete the project and not long afterward called Tom to say, "The state inspector advised us to request final inspection."

"I'll request it and call you tonight, Jay."

At seven Tom called, "Diamon is getting final approval of the project on Wednesday, the sixth of the month, at ten A.M. Make motel reservations for the general manager, my assistant and me. We're coming the day before."

Jay felt privileged to have the prominent company officials make the tour.

The following day, the state approved and accepted the entire project. They gave the company an award for being the number one contractor in the state.

Jay's special recognition read:

We award this honor to Engineer Jay Ryan: To a young, civil engineer with outstanding ability, knowledge, and dedication to honor the engineering profession.

The next day, Jay drove to the main office in Canon City. He gave Tom the pickup keys and asked him for a recommendation.

"You'll get a good one. Tonight come dressed for your farewell party at the country club. I'll pick you up at eight."

Jay was overwhelmed by the honors he received at the gala affair. Tom presented him with an engraved plaque in recognition of his outstanding work. John Wilmington presented him with a long envelope. When he opened it, Jay found the company had awarded him three and one-half months extra pay in recognition for each month he had shortened the timetable.

Jay said, "I never dreamed the job would be so rewarding. Thanks for giving me the opportunity to work for Diamon Construction Company."

At the end of the farewell party, Tom gave him a plane ticket to fly back to Grand Junction.

"Stay as long as you like. Just sign the hotel bill and we'll take care of it."

"I'll leave Saturday morning."

"Good luck, Jay, and God bless you."

"Thanks, Tom. It's been great working for you."

Carl came the next evening to ask Jay to come to dinner and to offer to take him to the airport on Saturday morning.

Back in his room, Jay called Margaret to see if she could meet his plane when he arrived the next day. She assured him she would be there. Then he called Miss Annie to see about a room. She said that would not be a problem.

In bed that night, Jay realized he had to make a decision regarding a job in South America with the Porvenir Construction Company. He must either take it or leave it.

# CHAPTER FIFTEEN

It was a somber James family that met Jay on Saturday morning. Carl shook his head sadly and said, "We sure hate to see you leave, Jay."

Tears began trickling down Jeffrey's cheeks faster than he could wipe them away. He asked, "Jay, since you're going to South America, will we ever see you again?"

"I hope so, Jeffrey," said Jay, smiling.

"But what if we don't?" Jeffrey persisted.

"You be your best self and don't forget me, okay?"

"I'll always remember you," said Jeffrey.

"And I will too," said Stephen.

After hugs and tears at the airport, Jay turned and joined those boarding the plane. When he looked around, he saw the family waving to him.

As the plane became airborne, he thought what a blessing he had received, as a result of a chance encounter with Carl, while coming to Canon City for a job interview.

He leaned back and relaxed. For a change it was nice to sit quietly and not have to be concerned or worried about what could go wrong. Soon he would see Margaret. It would be perfect if they were already married and he could take her with him.

He admired her self discipline and the goals she had set for herself. He was proud of her. She would make him a marvelous wife and she loved God the way he did.

He dozed off and slept until the stewardess said, "We'll soon be in the airport."

The instant the plane landed, Jay joined other passengers entering the terminal. He did not see Margaret and had started walking toward a phone to call her, when he heard, "Jay!"

Glancing around he saw her running toward him.

Embracing her he said, "Precious, I was getting worried."

"Sorry, I'm late. It's a busy time at the library."

"Let's get my luggage and put it in your car. I'll ride back with you. After I get some information from the travel agency, I'll meet you at the library. On your way home, will you take me to Miss Annie's boardinghouse?"

"Of course, I will."

"How did you find things at the library when you returned? Was the staff pleased we got engaged?"

"All except Mrs. Hargrove. She wasn't too kind in what she thought about me going to spend the weekend in Canon City. She implied my morals were such that the library should no longer let me work there."

"What did you say to her accusations, Margaret?"

"I told her I stayed in the home of a good family and you stayed in the hotel. I said you and I have high morals and we live by them. After telling her I had no desire to work where there was such suspicion and mistrust, I walked out and went home."

"Then what happened?"

"I heard the phone ringing when I entered the house. It was Mrs. Hargrove saying she had acted a bit hasty and I still had my job at the library."

"Good for you, Margaret."

"Now that we're engaged, I want to meet with your parents and ask for their consent. How about if I come to the house after I have dinner at Miss Annie's?"

"That would be fine, Jay."

At the travel agency, Jay got the lists and requirements for each country he planned to visit. When he returned to the library it was closed and Margaret was sitting in her car waiting for him.

"Let's drop your luggage off at Miss Annie's so she'll know you arrived, then stop by our favorite ice cream parlor to celebrate your homecoming."

"Great idea. What better place to go than where we had our first date?"

After they ordered, she snuggled close as Jay hugged her and asked, "Happy?"

"What a question! Though it saddens me to think of you leaving for South America."

"Let's put South America on hold," Jay said, caressing her hair and kissing her. "I want to cherish this moment and build up memories for when I'm far away and can't take you in my arms."

"You will call, won't you, Jay?"

"Yes, I promise to call every Saturday night despite the difference in time zones. Speaking of time, you better take me to Miss Annie's then get home to tell your parents about my visit tonight."

At the boardinghouse, he kissed her, got his luggage, and waved as she left.

The minute he rang the doorbell, Miss Annie called, "Come in, Jay. Your room's ready and so is dinner. You look great," she said, giving him a hug.

While they ate, he told her what had happened since he last saw her and about the honors he'd received. Then he said, "I'm saving the best news for last. Margaret Page and I are engaged."

"Congratulations! She's a fine young lady. I"m happy for both of you."

"Thanks, Miss Annie, for your good wishes and a super meal."

An hour later, Jay, sitting in one of Miss Annie's rockers on the porch, hurried to join Margaret when she stopped out front.

Upon arriving at her house that Saturday evening, Mr. and Mrs. Page gave him a warm welcome and said, "Let's go in the living room where it's comfortable."

Denis asked, "Are you gonna tell us a story about South America?"

"Sorry, not tonight. I have to take care of some important business," said Jay, smiling.

After everyone was seated, Jay rose, and faced Mr. and Mrs. Page. He said, "With all my respect, I am asking for your consent to marry your daughter in the near future."

Mr. Page said, "At that Sunday picnic, Ruth and I observed what a lovely couple you two made. We discussed it and prayed that if it was God's will for each of your lives it would work out. We can see it has and we welcome you into our family."

"Thank you. It's an honor I shall cherish," Jay said. The family hugged Jay and Margaret.

Mr. Page said, "Ruth, I don't believe we could have asked for a better husband for our daughter or a better son for us."

"Thanks," said Jay. "I feel fortunate to become a part of this caring family."

The next two weeks flew by so fast, Jay did not realize it was almost time for him to leave the United States, until Margaret asked if he had all his papers in order.

"I have the necessary papers and the company has forwarded my air fare. I'll call Enrique to tell him when I'll arrive so he can arrange for my interview with the company."

"Before I leave I must call Grandad. He'll be disappointed to hear I've accepted a job in South America. He was hoping I'd stay in this country."

"So was I," said Margaret.

After dinner that night, he called his grandfather.

"Grandad, I wanted to tell you I've accepted the South American job I was telling you about and I'll be flying down there this week. Also, I'm engaged to an attractive young lady named Margaret Page. She's looking forward to meeting you. When I return, I'll send you a round-trip ticket to attend our wedding."

"Sure hate to see you go, Son. Hoped you'd stay in this country and I could see you more often. Congratulations on your engagement, though." His voice breaking, he said, "I love you, Son. May the Lord watch over you."

"I love you, Grandad, and I'll try to write more often."

The days passed much too quickly and it was his last visit to the Page house, as he was flying the next day to Peru.

He and Margaret had spent a pleasant evening together with the family. Then, after the others retired, they sat at the dining room table, discussing their future plans before they had to be away from each other again.

"I'll call you every Saturday night," Jay promised.

"I'll be sitting by the phone waiting," said Margaret.

"Meantime, while I'm there working for our future, Margaret, have no fear of my love for you. I'm yours and I'll come back for you. I truly care for you."

"I care for you, Jay, but don't you think it would be better, once you've honored your commitment there, to look for work here? I hate to think of leaving my family to go live among strangers."

"They wouldn't be strangers long and you'd have me, Sweetheart. I'll do anything to make you happy. You're my life."

"Oh, Jay, I wish you would consider working in this country. Surely you could find a job here if you tried."

"Perhaps I could, but it wouldn't be as exciting as working in those countries."

"You talk as if you planned to spend your life there. I'm not sure that's what I want, at least not yet. Do you realize that if we moved to South America, I might seldom see my family ... might never see them once I leave the country?"

"Precious Margaret, don't get upset. There's plenty of time to work things out. Even if we did move there, you could fly back to see them. There might be times when I'd come with you. If I make good money, we could send them round-trip tickets to fly down and stay as long as they wanted. Please have patience and trust me to work things out for us, okay?"

"I'll think about it, Jay."

At the airport the next day, when the moment came to say good-by, Jay took her in his arms, held her close, looked into her beautiful eyes brimming with tears, and said, "If only I could take you with me, Precious. I would be the happiest man in the world, but I know I can't. Please wait for me, Sweetheart, so when we're married you can always be with me."

His own eyes misty, he kissed her again, and hurried to the plane. Torn between the desire to stay, yet knowing he must leave, it took all his resolve to go.

As the plane became airborne, his mind filled with various concerns, each crowding out the other. It was hard to believe the time had come to leave this wonderful land, knowing what lay ahead, it was even harder to accept the choice he had to make. He hoped it would not be a long separation and he could return to fulfill his promise to his beloved Margaret, the love of his life.

Though he had been away a long while, he became aware of the familiar landmarks of the South American countries they flew over. When the plane landed in Lima, Peru he did not realize the chubby man coming towards him in the terminal was Enrique.

Enrique recognized Jay at once and came running to give him a big hug.

"At last, I'm talking with Señor Enrique!" Jay exclaimed.

"You haven't changed a bit," said Enrique. "Let's claim your luggage and go to the house. Day after tomorrow, the Porvenir Construction Company wants you to report to their office."

As they drove along, Enrique asked, "So, you're not married?"

"No, I'm engaged to marry a young lady who has taken all of my heart, Enrique."

At the house, an attractive young woman with a toddler by her side, met them.

"Jay, this is Linda, my wife, and our two-year-old son, Arturo."

"This is the beautiful girl you were dating when I left South America."

"Make yourself at home, Jay. While we're waiting for dinner, let's go outside where you can relax and enjoy the pleasant view of our courtyard."

It was a delightful spot with the sun's last rays lighting up the well-landscaped area. A fountain with a cascading waterfall attracted birds to take a sip on their way to roost. They sat, each with his own thoughts, watching night come on. Enrique broke the silence.

"After years with no word from you, it's marvelous to see and talk with you again."

"I didn't know you were married until I got your letter saying you and Linda planned to vacation in Santiago, Chile."

"Until I toured your university, I had no idea what a difference quality schools make for students desiring to learn. Your excellent education, has helped you plot a course for a successful project."

"Enrique, we make a success or failure. Since graduation I've continued to spend time in research, reading, studying, and observing results others got in similar situations. While I was in the United States I took a course in rock work from one of their top mining schools. I'd be glad to share any information I've gained with you."

"Thanks. I'd appreciate it."

"What kind of engineering work are you doing?"

"I sub-contract with Constructora Ingenieros S. A. Jay, you may not like some things about the company you're going to work for."

Later, in bed, Jay wondered, was Enrique preparing him for the interview?

On Monday morning, he and Enrique went to the main office of Constructora Porvenir Ingenieros S. A. Enrique went along to introduce him to the receptionist.

"This is the engineer the company has been waiting for, Rosa," said Enrique.

"I shall introduce him to Señor Pablo Mendoza," she said.

"I am pleased, Señor Ryan, that you made it after months of inconvenience on our part. Please come in and meet our general manager, Señor Antonio Sanchez, and my assistant engineer, Señor Romulo Peña."

"I am honored," said Jay.

"Please be seated, Señor Ryan. Do you have a letter or recommendation from a company in your country where you worked?"

"Yes, it's a letter given to me when I finished a road project."

Pablo read the letter, then glanced at Jay. "It's hard to believe you are so capable. Are the people who signed this letter close friends of yours?"

"No. Tom Wood is the chief engineer and John Wilmington is the general manager of the company I worked for."

In a sarcastic tone, Pablo asked, "Does this mean the letter is based on fact?"

Stunned by what Pablo was implying, Jay's face reddened. His eyes took on a steely glint as he stared at Pablo, then in a stern voice replied, "Yes!"

Speaking in the same sarcastic tone, Pablo said, "Sorry, if my question has made you angry, Señor Ryan."

"If that was your purpose, you succeeded," said Jay.

Pablo said, "In order to become an employee, you must work six months to prove yourself to the company."

"Yes, I know and I'm happy because probation can work both ways."

"We shall take you to the personnel office to fill out the necessary papers for insurance and tax purposes. Señor Romulo will show you around this afternoon."

"Tomorrow morning we shall look at the projects and decide where you'll start."

After work, Jay called Enrique to pick him up. In Enrique's home, he was a different person.

Enrique asked, "Jay, what's wrong?

"Either the chief engineer has it in for me or he's setting me up for something."

The next day Pablo took Jay to several projects. Most had not been started. Back at the office, he asked, "Which one do you want?"

"That's up to you. Those I've seen offer little challenge. I'd enjoy something in solid rock with all kinds of problems."

The following day they drove to a mining camp over 13,000 feet above sea level in the high mountains. Still speaking in his same sarcastic tone Pablo said, "Señor Jay, the mining company wants a capable engineer to build a road all on solid rock. It's estimated to last seven months. They provide everything. You deal directly with them.We get a percentage of the cost to compensate the company."

Pablo introduced Jay to the chief engineer, Eric Adams.

They returned to Pablo's office and he said, "At eight tomorrow morning, I'll have a van take you and your belongings up to the mine."

That evening, Jay asked Enrique to take him shopping for some heavy work clothing.

Soon after he reached the project site where he was to build the road, he set up his work program and requested the equipment he needed to begin. His past experiences paid off. As a result of his skills and knowledge, in four months he finished the job and had it accepted. The mine signed a contract with the company for Jay to build another road.

He worked on the project up to the day his six-month probation ended. He called Señor Pablo to check the job. When he came, he admired Jay's work and marveled at what had been accomplished.

"This is incredible, Señor Jay. We'll have more of these projects for you."

"Not for me, Señor Pablo. My six months' probation period is up. I worked here to prove to you every word in my reference letter was true. You can have one of your engineers take over my job. I'll get my belongings and ride down with you."

At Pablo's office, Jay called Enrique to come for him.

When Enrique arrived, he asked, "What happened?"

"My six months of probation were up, so I took my option and quit."

"Are you going back to the United States?"

"No, I've been thinking about doing something different."

"What do you have in mind, Jay?"

"Selecting a large city that serves as headquarters for construction companies, and going into the consulting business for engineering and construction."

"Sounds like a great idea. Have you told Margaret?"

"No, I didn't want her to worry. She works part-time at the city library and is finishing her last year of college."

Jay spent several weeks searching out a suitable location for his business while he stayed in Enrique's home. Finally he found what he wanted in a city with a number of major construction companies.

That Saturday night when he called Margaret, he said, "Precious, the probation period was up, so I quit working for the company."

"Do you think you've made a wise decision?" Margaret asked.

"Yes, because of what I've learned. I've been checking out an idea of mine since I returned to South America. I've found a suitable location for our business, Ryan Engineering and Construction Consulting Office, in Santiago, Chile. I finalized all arrangements today."

"I'm so proud of you, Jay. I hope it works out."

"It will, Precious. I'm flying down there Monday to begin operation."

When Jay called Margaret on Saturday night from Santiago, he said, "Precious, I can't believe how well things are going. This is a setup that will bring work for years and provide us an excellent income. Remember Enrique, the friend I mentioned? I'm training him in rock work, so he can take over, when I need to be away. It doesn't seem possible that I will have been in South America for over eighteen months, by the time I come home for our wedding."

"It seems to me like you've been away forever."

"After we're married, Precious, I'll take you with me wherever I go. I want you by my side as I show you the beautiful city where we live."

"Jay, I hate to think about leaving and going to live in South America. I doubt I can do it."

"Well, Precious, you'll have me and I'll do everything I can to make you happy."

"I don't know, Jay. We'll talk about it when you get here."

After Jay put up the receiver, he thought, she can't be serious, but on the other hand, she could be. I love her so much I don't want to lose her.

The next Saturday he kept her talking and told her how much he loved her.

Not long afterward, Jay's consulting business suffered a terrible loss when Enrique, his business partner, was killed when something went wrong on the job.

Jay was devastated. What responsiblilty he had to Enrique's family. Overcome by grief, he managed to complete the job for the company, then hired an engineering student to keep a day log of telephone calls to the office.

On Satuday evening he called Margaret. and said, "Enrique was killed and I had to close down the operation."

"How terrible! Jay, that might have been you."

"Yes, Precious," Jay told her, his voice breaking.

Margaret didn't answer. Then he heard her sob and cry, "Oh, God!"

"Precious, are you all right?"

"The shock of Enrique's death has shown me how fast I could lose you. I want to be with you wherever you are for as long as we both shall live."

"You've made me the happiest man in the world."

"Hurry home, Jay."

The following week, as his plane landed in Grand Junction, Jay's heart pounded as he entered the terminal and saw Margaret waiting with the family.

"Jay!" She left them and ran to meet him.

"Precious, I thought this day would never come!"

Their tears of happiness mingled as they embraced and kissed each other.

While Jay and Margaret went to claim Jay's luggage, Mr. Page got a table where they could sit together. After they sat down, Jay said, "Let's thank God for bringing me home, then have a toast to our happiness as part of this caring family."

# CHAPTER SIXTEEN

As they left, Jay said, "Please drop me off at the board-inghouse."

"We'll leave your luggage, but you're having dinner with us," said Margaret.

At the Page home, the boys escorted Jay to a comfortable chair. Almost as soon as he sat down, he fell asleep. He awoke an hour later to find Margaret sitting beside him holding his hand.

"You must be exhausted, Jay," said Mrs. Page. "Dinner's ready. Soon as we eat, Margaret will take you to the board-inghouse where you can rest."

"Thanks, I'd appreciate it."

Jay managed to keep his eyes open through the meal and thank Mrs. Page.

As he kissed Margaret good night, he said, "Precious, I've pushed myself too much these past weeks. Once I get a good night's rest, I'll be a new man."

It was ten o'clock when Jay awoke the next day. He called Margaret at the library.

"I'll meet you at 12:30 if you can have lunch with me."

"Marvelous. Come early and chat a few minutes with the staff."

"Very well."

As they hurried to the restaurant, Jay said, "How we always scramble for time to talk. It's going to be great when we're married."

After lunch, Jay walked back to his room and took a nap.

That night at the Page home, they gathered in the living room and Jay asked, "Could we discuss plans for our wedding and set a date? I need to get back and take control of my consulting business. Margaret's and my future is there."

"We'll need three weeks," said Mrs. Page.

Mr. Page said, "Then we better decide today."

Glancing at Margaret and smiling, Jay said, "Since Margaret's finished college now, I think she should resign her library job and get ready to become Mrs. Ryan."

The next morning, Jay called Alaska State Ferry Office in Seattle, Washington, to inquire about a sailing date to Alaska and the availability of stateroom for two on the Ferry.

"Sir, we have a sailing date for the second day of the month at eight A.M. and there is only one stateroom available."

"Book the round-trip and stateroom for my wife and me. I'll call you back at two P.M. and transfer the money."

"That night when Jay and Mr. Page were alone, he told him what he had planned as a surprise for Margaret. They would fly to Seattle, spend the night in a hotel and board the ferry for their six-day honeymoon in Alaska. "Keep it a secret," he said.

At dinner, Jay said, "Please plan for the wedding to be on the last day of the month." Then he added, "I want to visit Grandad and get him to fly back with me. If I'm there, I can help with what he needs to have done before he leaves."

Later, in his room, Jay called his grandfather to say he was coming to spend a few days with him. "Then we'll fly back together and you'll be here for the wedding."

"I'll count the hours 'til you get here, Son."

When Jay arrived at the ranch, he looked around and said, "While I'm here, I want to help you make the improvements you've been wanting to make. We'll hire the best well driller in the area to drill a deep well to get water for irrigation and piping to the house and barn. Then we'll hire plumbers and electricians to put in a bathroom and check the wiring. Whatever needs to be done to improve the house, we'll get it done."

"Impossible, Son. It will cost too much!"

"No, it won't. It's something I've always wanted to do for you."

"Okay, Son. I assure you, it will be appreciated."

"As we proceed, Grandad, I'll need your suggestions and help in finding qualified people for the work."

"No problem, Son. I know everybody."

A couple days later, the ranch was like a busy air terminal with people coming and going. Jay kept busy supervising and working with the carpenters, electricians, and plumbers. Grandad watched the well drilling with interest. When water began flowing, he took off his Stetson hat, threw it up in the air, and shouted, "Thank you, Lord!"

After ten days, working from daylight to dark, they finished the job. What a difference it made in the look and comfort of the house. Even the barn had electric lights.

Jay called Margaret to say he and Grandad would arrive the next day at four P.M.

"Please be there to meet us, Precious."

Then he called Miss Annie to be sure she had a room for his grandfather.

After dinner on his last day at the ranch, Jay said, "Let's watch the sunset, then get to bed, for we fly to Grand Junction tomorrow."

The next day, when they arrived at the airport and entered the terminal, Margaret was waiting. Jay introduced Grandad Bill to her and they got along so well together, he was delighted.

At the boardinghouse, Margaret said, "I'll see you later and take you to the house for dinner."

Grandad said, "Margaret, please excuse me, but I need to stay in and rest tonight."

"Very well, we'll see you tomorrow night and no excuses."

The following day was special for Grandad. Jay took him shopping and bought him two suits with accessories. Then they each got a haircut. After they dressed and were waiting for Margaret, Jay teased, "Grandad, you don't look like the same man. You're handsome in that dark suit with that tie."

"Thanks, Son. I admire our taste."

When Margaret came for them, she kissed Jay then hugged his grandfather.

He smiled and told her, "Now I feel like I'm your grandad."

At the Page home, it was evident that Margaret and her family enjoyed him. They listened and asked questions about life on the ranch. Denis and Frank, one on each side, held his hands like they were his own grandchildren. He kept everyone entertained with exploits of Jay's father when he was a boy. Jay leaned forward, so as not to miss a word, and learned things he never knew.

Watching the facial expressions of the family members, as they were involved in what Grandad was saying, Jay had to admit that his grandfather was a master storyteller. He knew how to spin a good yarn and hold peoples' attention.

Dinner was a pleasant affair with everyone joining in with interesting table talk.

As they were leaving for the boardinghouse, Margaret's parents told Grandad, "We have enjoyed the time with you and want you to come to dinner every night with Jay."

"Thanks," said Grandad. "Your kindness makes me feel I'm in a different world."

Taking his hand, Denis looked up at him and asked, "Do you mind if Frank and I call you Grandad? You'll be kin to us when Jay marries Margaret."

Grandad smiled. Putting his arms around their shoulders, he said,"Boys, I'm happy to have you for my grandchildren. From here on call me Grandad Bill."

Passing the post office, Margaret said, "The wedding invitations have been mailed. If they all attend, we'll have quite a crowd."

Everyone worked to help get things ready for the wedding. Jay had no idea it would entail so much planning and effort. Mrs. Page fretted about the food, wondering if there would be enough. When Jay named his favorite cake, she baked it for the groom's cake. The wedding cake recipe was one that had been in the family for generations.

Prior to the wedding, there were rehearsals at the church, dinners given by friends for the happy couple, and the special dinner given by Margaret's parents for members of the wedding party and honored guests. Though Jay found he stayed busy and on the go, he looked forward to each day with the expectancy and delight of a small child at Christmas time.

At last the day came. At the church, Jay could not believe the large crowd waiting to hear them say their vows. It was a solemn and sacred occasion, one of the most beautiful of his life, Jay thought. He waited for the moment when he would see his beautiful bride in the lovely wedding dress she had designed and created.

He watched Denis lighting the candles, making sure each one burned before going to the next. How could this young boy act as if he did this every day, while Jay felt his heart pounding and his throat dry? Was it something that plagued all grooms?

He was happy Grandad was best man. The idea occurred to him at the ranch, but he did not want to say anything until he discussed it with Margaret. Unfortunately, he never got around to doing it.

After Margaret told him she had selected her maid of honor and bridesmaids, she said, "If you don't have someone in mind for your best man, I think Grandad would be perfect."

"So do I, if we can get him to agree," said Jay.

As those thoughts flitted through his mind, he glanced at Grandad, the picture of serenity.

Grandad winked and whispered, "Wait 'til you see your bride. You've never seen her as radiant and beautiful as she will appear today."

When the organist began the wedding march and the crowd stood, Jay gazed in awe and admiration as Margaret, escorted by her father, entered. As he watched her proceed down the aisle toward him, he had to admit that Grandad was right. My beloved bride could not look lovelier.

Everything went according to plan, but Jay only saw Margaret. He was thankful a professional photographer was taking pictures they could view later.

At last came the most beautiful moment of his life, Jay embraced his bride, gave her a gentle kiss, then turned to receive congratulations and best wishes from the crowd.

Later, after the cake had been cut and while their guests were enjoying the food and conversation, Jay and Margaret slipped away to change into their travel clothes and leave in the taxi Mr. Page had called.

After they left, Grandad thanked Mr. and Mrs. Page for their kindness and said he had made reservations to leave next morning. Russ would take him to the airport.

Meanwhile, Jay and Margaret had caught a flight to Seattle, Washington. After spending the night there, they boarded the ferry on their honeymoon to Alaska. Jay knew she was pleased with his surprise, when a passenger yelled, 'Thar she blows!' A majestic gray whale surfaced and gave a performance for the onlookers.

"They're such magnificient creatures. I'm happy I'm getting to see them," she said.

For the remainder of the voyage, she became an avid whale watcher.

After a brief stay in historic Sitka, they returned to Grand Junction to write and thank friends for wedding gifts; sort and get things packed for shipment to South America.

A few nights before they were to leave, Margaret told Jay, "I never realized how hard it would be to go far away from my famly. I want to enjoy them as long as I can."

"Sweetheart," said Jay, taking her in his arms and kissing her, "I'll do my best to make you happy, now and always."

The night before they were to fly out, Jay called his grandfather. "Grandad, we're flying down to Santiago, Chile tomorrow. I don't know when we'll have a chance to get back, but hang in there and enjoy the ranch. I promise the first time I can be away, I'll bring Margaret to see how nice the ranch looks. Keep up your cooking skills, as I've told her it's worth a trip to the States to sample your sourdough bread and biscuits."

"Take care, Son and you and Margaret have a safe trip. Try to write."

"We will, Grandad. We love you."

The morning they were to leave, the family escorted them to the airport. After fond farewells, they boarded the plane and found their seats in the first class section. As they waited, they heard the announcement, "Passengers bound for South America will change planes at Los Angeles. Check your passports and all papers required by the countries you are visiting."

They stayed in Los Angeles overnight in order to leave at six A.M. and see some of South America during daylight hours. It was a fourteen-hour flight with a stop-over in Lima, Peru. By eight P.M., they would reach the Santiago International Airport, their final destination.

They had been flying a short time, when the stewardess brought them a tempting array of foods for breakfast, a treat the airline offered once each month to passengers flying first class.

Sitting by the window, Margaret asked, "What is that land to the left of the plane?"

"The Panama Canal Zone. It's an engineering project our country succeeded in making a success."

Shortly, the pilot of the plane stopped by and asked if their destination was Lima, Peru or Santiago, Chile.

"Santiago," said Jay. "I have a consulting business there that provides technical help to contractors. It's where we hope to make our home."

"Great! Would you two like to visit the cockpit of my plane? It's been built especially for long flights with bunks and plenty of room to stretch out and read. An aircraft like this one can almost fly by itself. Takeoff, landing, and turbulent weather are about the only times we have to work."

"Yes, thanks. We would enjoy seeing it," said Jay, as he and Margaret followed him.

In the cockpit, Jay said, "It doesn't resemble what I had in front of me when I flew."

Margaret stared at the equipment for an instant, then looked beyond to the panoramic view from the window. Enjoying themselves, they stayed so long, Jay apologized.

He asked the captain if when they were nearing Santiago Margaret could return to the cockpit to take a peek at the city.

"Yes. I'll have her escorted here at that time."

As the plane touched down at Lima, Peru International Airport, the passengers heard, "We have landed to refuel.

You'll have some time to visit this modern airport with its shopping center and all merchandise is tax free."

Jay and Margaret found a section of small stores featuring souvenirs like llama and alpaca rugs and assorted jewelry items made of either 18 karat gold or pure silver. Margaret was interested in selecting some small rugs. Jay told her to get what she wanted, while he looked at the jewelry.

Back at the plane, the stewardess gave them special Peruvian souvenir bags to show they had purchased the items in Lima and would not need to pay when they went through customs in Chile.

After several hours flight, a stewardess escorted Margaret to the cockpit.

"Please sit down in the folding chair between my seat and the copilot's, Mrs. Ryan.

We're approaching Santiago. Captain to Control Tower, please indicate if I can circle once over the city."

"There is no aircraft in the region. Permission granted"

After he did so, the captain came in for a landing, following instructions from the control tower.

The instant the plane touched down, Margaret exclaimed, "That was fantastic!" She went to where Jay was sitting, threw her arms around him, and cried, "I saw it all!"

As they were leaving, the captain stood at the door of the cockpit and asked, "What did you think of all this, Mrs. Ryan?"

"Captain, it's too marvelous for words," she replied. "Something I'll never forget."

The captain held out his hand and said, "Here's my card. It's been great meeting and talking with you two. Some evening when my flight stays here overnight, I'd like to visit with you."

"Thanks," Jay said, taking his card. "Here's mine with all our information. When you are staying over, call and we'll meet you at the airport. Thanks for your kindness."

That night Jay and Margaret stayed at the Hotel Regent in Santiago.

He called his office the next morning and told the engineering student to have his pickup serviced and be at the hotel with it the following day at ten A.M.

At breakfast the first morning in the hotel, Jay said,"There's something I want to tell you. It concerns the time when I had to leave South America after losing everything I had earned. I wept as I looked back at the countries that had taken part of my heart. Yet, despite what happened, I had hopes of returning someday. However, I had no idea that God would include an adoring wife to return with me."

Margaret smiled. "God always gives us more than we ask for."

After lunch, Jay said, "While we're driving around this afternoon, I have a surprise I want to show you."

"I'm curous. What is it?"

"If I tell you, it won't be a surprise, so you'll have to wait and see," Jay teased.

In a short while, he turned onto a street that led to a house set in a wooded area.

"Why don't you look around, while I wait for the realtor who's meeting us here?"

"I will," said Margaret.

When she returned a few minutes later, she said, "I saw two deer feeding and fish swimming in the river."

As they talked, a car parked by Jay's pickup. A man got out and motioned for them to follow him up the walk.

Inside the house they went through the rooms discussing possibilities for making it the kind of home they wanted. They agreed to meet the realtor in his office the next afternoon.

On the way back to the hotel, Jay asked, "What do you think? Do you like it?"

"I love the location and the way the house is constructed, it has the potential for a nice home. However, don't you think it's a bit large for the two of us?"

"No," Jay grinned, "even if it seems large for us now, in years to come, we might need the space. I hope we have a daughter exactly like you, and if God blesses us with more than one, it's fine with me."

"Jay, I hope we have little boys the image of you."

"You see," said Jay, grinning, "with a future-oriented viewpoint, the house is perfect."

The next afternoon, he made an offer. It was accepted and they were given the keys. He asked the realtor to call the telephone company and have the phone activated with their name, using Jay's company office for mailing.

That night Margaret called her parents. "Guess what, we've bought a house in a lovely location."

The next morning Jay said, "With my work, I won't have time to take you wherever you need to go to get the things you need. While I'm downtown today, I'll buy you a car."

"Thanks, Jay. It will be a big help to have my own transportation."

They lived at the hotel for several weeks, while some small contracting companies they hired did the remodeling work.

Involved with his consulting business, Jay left the supervisory details to Margaret. She knew enough Spanish to make herself understood. After his first inspection when the house was a mess with all the remodeling, he found no time to check on it again. When he thought to ask Margaret how work was progressing, she said, "It's coming along."

Tired of living in the hotel, he was ready to suggest they move to the house even if it wasn't finished. As he left, Margaret said, "When you leave the office this afternoon, come by there and give me your idea on something."

"What's wrong?"

"I can't explain. Once you see it, you'll know what to do."

"I hope it's not complicated. I think I could have built a new house faster."

Later, in the office, Jay had difficulty keeping his mind centered on his consulting business. He hoped it wasn't a structural problem as he liked the current arrangement of the house.

As he drove out that afternoon he reproached himself for neglecting to check with Margaret earlier to see if she needed his input. He could understand why she would solve a problem herself rather than bother him with it.

When he reached the house, he was surprised to find the worker's gone and only Margaret's car parked nearby. What did they mean by leaving at such an early hour? They had seemed responsible when he hired them. Jumping out of the pickup and slamming the door shut, in three leaps, he was at the door. Yanking it open, he strode down the dimly-lit hall toward a beam of light, yelling, "Margaret!"

"Here I am, Jay. Your timing is perfect. We'll eat soon as I serve dinner."

Surprised, Jay stood as if his feet were set in concrete. He watched as Margaret brought in delicious-looking and good-smelling bowls of food and placed them on a table set for two.

"Margaret, I didn't know you knew how to prepare these kind of meals. I thought brides learned to cook after they got married."

"Not in my family," Margaret told him. "I learned how to prepare food and serve it attractively at an early age."

"Precious, you amaze me with what you've accomplished," Jay said, kissing her as she passed by.

"It you think this is something, wait until you see the other rooms."

"You mean they're finished and we can move in?"

"Everything's in place except our luggage, and we can get that at the hotel tomorrow."

Taking her in his arms and kissing her tenderly, Jay said, "God sure blessed me when he made you my beloved wife."

# EPILOGUE

What happens to Jay Ryan and his loved ones in the future?

Jay meets Margaret at the house they are remodeling expecting to help her solve a critical problem. He is overwhelmed when he enters to find everything in place and Margaret ready to serve his favorite foods on a beautifully set table for two.

He finds she is full of surprises, doing things to make him happy and enjoy their time together. They like to entertain guests and since Jay knows people from his days in the university and work, they exchange dinners with other couples.

By end of the second year in Santiago, Margaret is ready to deliver her first child. Jay sends her mother a round trip ticket to fly down for the event. She arrives the week that baby Ruth Ann, named for both Margaret's and Jay's mothers, is born.

Margaret has ample household help which gives her mother free time to enjoy her first grandchild, a few days before she returns to Grand Junction with photos to show Stanley and the boys.

Two years later, Jay Leon Ryan is born. Jay feels so blessed, he wants to share his happiness and sends Margaret's parents and brothers round trip plane tickets to fly down for a visit.

The following year, they get a letter from Grandad Bill saying he would really like to see them. Jay said, "I'd like to go, but it would be too hard on the children."

"No, it won't. Let's go," Margaret tells him.

The next morning, Jay begins getting things in order for them to fly out at the earliest to spend time with Grandad on his West Texas cattle ranch.

Now that he is a family man with a wife and children who adore him, Jay no longer is the impulsive person looking for dangerous adventures.

# BIOGRAPHY

Marie Avant earned a M.Ed. degree from Central Washington State University. Prior to retirement, she worked in Eastern Washington and later served as Washington State University Area Extension Agent in Western Washington. She also held an associate professor title.

During this period she had the experience of doing daily radio and television programs, as well as news writing for a daily and weekly newspaper in the two-county area where she taught. She edited a consumer information newsletter; trained leaders to present consumer educational materials to off-campus classes; was a speaker for various professional, educational, and church groups; and was privileged to work with three Indian tribes in the family living program.

She has been published in two poetry anthologies and her articles and stories have been published in Christian magazines for adults and children.

To order additional copies of:

*Passage to Peru*

please send $12.99 plus $3.95 shipping and handling to:

WinePress Publishing
P.O. Box 1406
Mukilteo, WA 98275

or have your credit card ready and call:

1-800-917-BOOK